The cowboy knocked on her door. "Dammit, Holly, what you doing?"

"What the hell you think I'm doing?" she hollered. "Go

But he was on the floor to protest.

TR sat up in bed, pulled back the hammer of his Colt and shot the intruder twice, and once more as he lay on the floor.

Holly said, "Jesis! Didja have to shoot 'im?"

The body lay half in the hall. TR slid out of bed and grabbed his jeans. He yanked them up and shoved into his boots.

The saloon downstairs was suddenly quiet. Bootheels sounded on the steps. In the hall a man's voice said, "Billy!"

TR heard click-clack as the man thumbed the hammer of his revolver. He said, "You—in the room—come out here."

TR ducked down low as Holly began to babble in fear. He paid no attention but crept close to the body in the doorway.

The man outside repeated, "You inside there—come on out."

Also by Arthur Moore
Published by Fawcett Books:

THE KID FROM RINCON
TRAIL OF THE GATLINGS
THE STEEL BOX
DEAD OR ALIVE
MURDER ROAD
ACROSS THE RED RIVER
THE HUNTERS

THE OUTLAWS

Arthur Moore

FAWCETT GOLD MEDAL • NEW YORK

A Fawcett Gold Medal Book
Published by Ballantine Books
Copyright © 1991 by Arthur Moore

Library of Congress Catalog Card Number: 91-91815

ISBN 0-449-14657-X

Manufactured in the United States of America

First Edition: May 1991

Chapter One

The U.S. government's disburser in Kansas City was on vacation. It was the beginning of spring and his assistant, Daniel Evans, was in charge of the office. Evans was a small, dark man with an eternally crabbed expression. It was said of him that he had never been known to smile. His wife said to her close friends that he had not even smiled on his honeymoon. He was also a pinchpenny.

When the allotment for the Indian reservation, Santa Cruz, came across his desk, Evans was aghast. One hundred and fifty thousand dollars was to be delivered to the Indian agent there. The voucher was properly made out and signed. He could find no fault with it.

The money was to be delivered in cash.

Evans brooded about it all day and told his wife at supper that night. One hundred and fifty thousand dollars in cash! The crazy fools in Washington were throwing our tax money away!

His wife, named Nattie, seldom agreed with anything he said or did. But after seven years of marriage and a thousand spats, she kept that knowledge from him. She made the best of her situation and put a little aside when she was able, out of the household fund.

It was a week after Evans had mentioned the reservation allotment that Nattie's brother, Marty Nevers, stopped by the house as he was passing through Kansas City. Marty was older and the black sheep of the family. It was said that Marty ran with Matt Moody, the notorious outlaw.

Marty looked very fine, respectable even, dressed in new store clothes with a gold watch chain across his middle. He and Nattie sat down for coffee in the parlor.

As a matter of course they discussed the family, though Marty was not much interested in the topic. But when she mentioned the reservation money, his eyes lighted up. She knew very little about it, however. It would be in cash, according to her husband, and would be sent from the federal building to the train, then transferred to a stage and taken to the reservation.

Marty made a joke about it, told her he was on his way east, asked her not to tell Evans he had stopped by . . . and went to the door.

She said, "I don't tell him ever'thing I know."

He kissed her cheek and left.

The shipment to the Indian agent, Mr. Harbourg, was well marked with big black letters. The greenbacks were packed into a stout wooden box painted dark blue. The box had four iron straps around it and was fastened with a heavy padlock. The markings read: PROPERTY OF THE U.S. GOV'T. CONSIGNED TO SANTA CRUZ RES.

It was very heavy.

Marty Nevers sat in a window across the street from the federal building. He watched with binoculars as a green express wagon drew up to the side door and several men carried out boxes and stowed them in the panel wagon. He easily spotted the iron-bound box marked "Santa Cruz."

He followed the wagon to the train depot and was able to get very close. He made certain the blue box was put into the train baggage car. Then he sent a wire to Matt Moody in Hayestown and boarded the same train west.

It took the train two days to arrive at the little whistle-stop named Wilkins. Matt and three others were there: Clell, T.R., and Lem Bowman. They lounged on the platform and watched as the box and other goods were loaded into a stage-coach boot which was surrounded by five heavily armed uni-formed guards.

Matt asked Marty, "How much is in the box?"

"One hundred and fifty thousand in cash."

Matt whistled softly.

Marty, still in respectable store clothes, bought a ticket and boarded the stagecoach with several others, ostensibly bound for Durham in the south. When the stage moved out, it was followed closely by the five guards.

And followed at a distance by Matt and the gang.

It was a dreary journey, south and west; the stage moved steadily all day long with short stops every hour or two, and a longer stop at a way station.

Near nightfall the stage rolled into Elland, a small burg built up around the stage station. The passengers were in-formed they would spend the night in one of the tiny rooms provided. The stage would then go on, scheduled to reach Elk Hill the next night.

There was a short bar built into the restaurant wall, and after supper Marty had a drink, one foot on the rail. He asked the bartender, "Isn't there an Indian reservation somewhere near here?"

He looked surprised. "You want to go there?"

"Hell, no. I was just curious. But the stage don't stop there?"

"Naw. The stage goes on south. The reservation is west from here."

Marty nodded, looked at his watch, and finished his drink. He wandered out into the cool night. That meant the money box would be loaded onto another wagon to go to the reser-vation. He lit a cigar and walked out to the road. It was time to meet Matt. He waited only a short time till the other showed up, grinning at him in the night.

Marty said, "I better come with you tonight, Matt." He repeated what the barman had told him.

"All right. You got any luggage back there?"

"Nothing I want."

Matt said, "They going to ask questions in the morning when you don't show up."

"That's a hell of a shame," Marty said and got up on the horse behind Matt.

The four others in the gang had made camp in a valley a mile east of the station. They welcomed Marty and gave him coffee while he told them what he knew.

"The stage will go on south, but they got to load the agent's box onto a buckboard, prob'ly, and take it west to the reservation."

"We'll be watchin'," Clell said.

"There's five guards."

"Five or forty," Matt said. "We ambush the wagon and too bad if they git in the way. The best time is before they get settled. As soon's they turn off the stage road, we hit 'em hard. Shoot the horses and stop 'em right there. What you say, Marty?"

"That's good. They won't have time t'think."

Lem said, "They'll prob'ly go damn early. . . ."

"So we'll git there earlier."

It went exactly as planned in the morning. There was a shallow arroyo close to the turnoff road. They corralled the horses a short distance away and slid into the arroyo with rifles before first light.

When the reservation buckboard arrived from the station with the five horsemen, Clell and Lem Bowman shot the team mules, and the wagon bumped to a halt. A fusillade knocked three men from the saddles—but two galloped away over the plain.

The gunmen unhooked the dead mules, pulled the wagon away, and backed two horses into the shafts. Marty mounted the third horse, and the gang went south with the wagon and the blue treasure box.

"Hell, there wasn't nothing to it," Matt said, and Marty grinned back.

Chapter Two

JOHN Fleming, Chief of Security Operations, West, met Laredo and Pete Torres in Kansas City in the Chandler Hotel bar. Fleming was just coming off a two-week rest that he had spent in Kansas visiting relatives.

The room was nearly deserted at that hour, and Fleming's cigar made the air blue. He said, "You've probably read in the papers about Matt Moody . . . ?"

Laredo nodded. "It's suspected he just held up a reservation cash shipment. Is it true?"

"We think it is. It has Moody's stamp on it. He's ambushed other shipments exactly the same way."

Pete asked, "Any witnesses?"

"Two of the reservation guards got away with slight wounds, as the newspapers report. But neither of them saw anything. It happened suddenly and unexpectedly. Neither of them had time to fire a weapon."

"Too bad . . ."

"But we've talked to several witnesses who describe a man on the stagecoach who we're positive was Martin Nevers. We have a photograph of him taken in jail, and the witnesses all pointed him out."

"He was on the stagecoach that carried the money box?"

"Yes. We think Marty learned of the shipment somehow, right in this city. We've got detectives working on that angle. It may have been an inside job. Maybe he paid off someone in the Bureau of Indian Affairs. Very few knew of the shipment, of course. Those things are always kept as secret as possible."

Laredo rubbed his chin. He was a tawny-haired young giant with regular, square features. He was dressed conservatively in a dark blue suit; the coat seemed to be stretched across his shoulders, and his shirt buttons threatened to pop off. He said, "Then you think Marty Nevers followed the shipment west and somehow met up with Matt Moody and the rest of them?"

"Exactly." Fleming puffed his cigar. He was a large, paunchy man whose coat sleeves had tiny burn holes from his incessant cigar smoking. "That's what we think, yes. Of course, we have no details. But we want the money back."

Pete Torres was also a big man, maybe slightly larger than Laredo, and dressed in a pearl-gray suit. He was dark, with hair black and shiny. He was a top-of-the-class graduate, as was Laredo, of the Tanner Training Center near Springfield. They had met at the school and had been posted one, two in a class of twenty. They were now members of the elite Bluestar Unit. The Tanner Organization did work almost exclusively for the government.

Pete asked, "You want us to bring in Matt Moody?"

Fleming put down the cigar. "Let me tell you what the government feels. Everyone is fed up with Matt Moody. He has robbed too goddamn many government shipments and killed too many agents. This reservation affair is the last damn straw. We want Matt Moody dead or alive—preferably dead—and his entire gang with him. Yes, we want you to bring him in under his own power or slung over the back of a horse dead as a man can get. We don't really care which."

Pete grinned. "That's pretty clear."

"It's not for publication," Fleming warned, waving the cigar. "To the reporters, we say that Moody is a menace and we will put a stop to him and his depredations. To you, I say track him down and shoot the son of a bitch." He puffed the cigar. "I never said that."

6

Laredo smiled. "We get the idea. And now we want to know everything we can about him."

"He is not married. We know he sends money to his mother who lives in the little town of Peryton, and he has been seen there infrequently. She is locally famous as his mother. Moody enjoys a sort of Robin Hood reputation, strangely enough. He is anything but. However, he has apparently fostered the notion—Moody is no fool. He is about forty-three and has a slash birthmark across his left cheek that cannot be disguised easily. It stands out prominently in daylight." He opened a folder. "Here are prison pictures of him and three of the gang."

He passed them across. Moody had thick brows that met in the middle, and his expression was glowering. He wore a heavy black mustache, and the birthmark was very evident.

Laredo studied the photograph of Clell Timmins. He was a young man, maybe in his mid-twenties, dark and good-looking, with a slight smile on his smooth face.

Fleming said, "Timmins is a fancy dresser. He likes girls and spends money lavishly on them. He has no family, and he is a killer. We think he likes it."

The picture of Marty Nevers showed a square-faced man who looked to be about forty. He was dark, with a smaller mustache but no marks.

Fleming pointed to the photo. "Nevers is mean as a snake. He's also unmarried and is fast with a gun. Take no chances with him."

The photograph of Toby Rogers showed a slim young man, clean-shaven and almost baby-faced. Fleming tapped the picture. "They call him T.R., and he's quick and good with a gun. We're sure he's killed six men."

He had no picture of Lem Bowman. "He's never been in a jail that took pictures. He is married, but we don't know where his wife is. He is exceptionally good with a rifle, and they say he doesn't talk much. You can keep the pictures."

Laredo asked, "Where would we start looking for them?"

"They have two hangouts we know about, one in Hayes-town and the other in Camp Hill. Both are little burgs with no law. We know they have gone to both to rest up and have fun between jobs. Hayestown is not far from the spot they robbed the reservation money.''

"Interesting . . ."

"I'll try to find more information for you. Keep me posted where you are.''

Pete asked, "How many have gone after Moody?''

"Quite a few, including some U.S. marshals. Moody spent a few years in a territorial prison when he was younger. He was arrested drunk five years ago, but his gang broke him out before he went to trial. Moody likes to drink.''

They decided to go first to Hayestown and rode in at night. As Fleming had said, the town was a tiny collection of shacks, saloons, and dance halls, and not much else. It was located across the river from the large town of Ackland. Although the two towns were connected by a long wooden bridge, they were situated in different counties, and the law in Ackland turned a blind eye to the many sins of Hayestown.

Laredo and Pete joined the considerable traffic across the long bridge. Obviously the citizens of Ackland visited the pleasure palaces of Hayestown in numbers. It was the middle of the evening and the saloons were going full blast, the dance halls overflowing.

No one gave them a second glance.

However, Laredo thought it might be a mistake to ask for Matt Moody. It would certainly draw attention to them.

"Then let's ask for one of the others,'' Pete suggested.

They entered the largest saloon in town and found it bustling. In the back of the saloon was a stage where a band was playing and girls in tights were dancing. Laredo got the bartender's attention.

"D'you know if Clell Timmins is in town?''

The other gave him a hard look. "You know 'im?''

"He's my cousin.''

The barman nodded, then looked around the room. "Be right back.''

Laredo watched him beckon to one of the painted girls

8

and lean over the bar to talk with her. He pointed out Laredo, and she studied him, nodded, and in a moment came toward him.

"You Clell's cousin?"

"Yes. On my mother's side. Is he here?"

"He never mentioned a cousin to me. . . ."

He smiled. "Well, I never talk about him either."

She pursed her lips. "Yeh, I guess I don't know half my cousins neither." She was dressed in saloon finery, and she was well made up. She's probably older than she looks, he thought. She never looked directly at him, her eyes kept sliding off and returning. She said, "What's your name?"

"Fred Burns. What's yours?"

"Cora."

He asked, "Is Clell in town?"

"Yeh, he is. He's over at Charlie's place. You know where that is?"

"No."

"All right. I'll get Donny to show you." She turned away and paused. "You stay here, huh?"

He agreed, and she went toward the back of the saloon, disappearing in the crowd. Laredo nodded to Pete, who leaned on the bar several paces away.

Cora was back in about ten minutes with a younger man, poorly dressed, with lank brown hair, and no chin. She said, "This's Donny. He'll show you."

"Thanks."

Donny said, "Let's go thisaway." He threaded his way through the crowd to a door beside the theater stage. It led to a hall, then to a back door and steps down to the dark alley where there were half a dozen horses in a picket line and barrels of trash. Donny led the way down the alley for a short distance then climbed a low fence and halted.

"You'n Clell know each other by sight?"

"Yes, of course," Laredo said. "But I haven't seen him for a while. Has he changed any?"

"Naw. He'll never change much. Still the same slick dresser." Donny pointed. "He's in that house there. You jus'

9

go knock on the door." He went back across the fence and hurried away.

Laredo watched him go. When he had disappeared in the dark, Pete came across the fence. "What did he tell you?"

"He said Clell's in that house."

Pete glanced around and made a face. "This feels like a trap. You think they believed that cousin story?"

"Maybe not. I wonder if there's another door. That's a pretty small house."

"I'll go look." Pete edged around the little house and returned in a moment, shaking his head.

Laredo picked up a stick, motioned to Pete to stand aside, and stepped to the door. Reaching out, he rapped on it with the stick. Instantly there was a booming crash, and a large jagged hole appeared in the middle of the door. Someone had fired a shotgun!

In the next moment the door opened, and a man looked out, a pistol in his hand. He peered at the ground, evidently expecting to see a body. Then he glanced up, saw Laredo's shadowy figure, and fired.

Laredo fired back, and the man crumpled. He stumbled down the steps and fell sprawling as the revolver clattered away.

Laredo advanced, pistol ready, but no one came from the house. He knelt and turned the body over, moving the head so the mealy light from the house fell full on Clell Timmons's features.

Pete asked, "Is he dead?"

"Yes, I'm afraid so."

Pete went up the steps and slipped into the house. He was gone only a minute and came out holstering his Colt. "No one in there. It was a trap, all right. I expect they thought you were the law."

"Looks like it."

Laredo stood, poked out the brass, and reloaded. Pete went to the fence, listening. "I think they're coming this way."

They went back over the fence as men came from the

saloon, talking loudly. They had heard the shots. Laredo looked back once at the body and shook his head. A clumsy trap . . .

In the shadowy main street they mounted and rode slowly back across the rickety bridge to Ackland. There was now one less of the Moody gang.

Pete said, "That girl in the saloon—she didn't trust you."

"Maybe she knew Clell had no cousins."

"Yes, that was probably it. They're a hair-trigger bunch." Laredo agreed. "And they'll be worse now."

Chapter Three

THE death of Clell Timmins caused no stir at all. It was effectively covered up—by someone. No notice got out to the Ackland *Weekly Dispatch*.

Laredo wired John Fleming, in code, telling him of the incident, and Fleming wired back saying it might be best to leave matters at that. It would serve no purpose to spread the death over the papers. He had no new information for them.

Pete said, "Why don't we try something different—since we need information. Why not advertise for it?"

Laredo's brows went up. "Advertise for information about Matt Moody?"

"Exactly. Offer to pay for it."

"Would anyone dare answer?"

"How do we know unless we try it?"

Laredo chuckled. "All right. Let's go talk to the people at the newspaper."

The Ackland *Weekly Dispatch* was housed on a side street, the offices in front and the composing room and presses in the back. The sign outside informed passersby that job printing was also done to order at reasonable prices.

A skinny, cigar-smoking clerk met them at a counter, and Laredo wrote out the ad: Cash for information concerning Matt Moody. Strictly confidential. No names.

The clerk read the ad and stared at them. "Are you lawmen?"

12

"In a way," Laredo replied. "Do you have a box number to attach to the ad?"

"Yes. But I never heard of the law advertising like this."

"It's the age of invention," Pete said.

The clerk frowned at him.

Laredo said, "When will the ad come out?"

"With the next edition, in three days." The clerk took the payment, still shaking his head.

They went out to the walk, and Pete rolled a cigarette. "What if we get no answers?"

"Then we'll try something else. Maybe Fleming will send us something."

The newspaper came out on time, but it was several days before they received an answer. A sealed note was delivered to the box. How much did they offer for information? The note suggested they leave an answer with the local priest, Father Julian.

The Catholic church was in a run-down building off the main street in the center of town. When they called on the priest, he knew about the note. Father Julian was an older man, very gray, and almost feeble. He received them in a tiny, cluttered office.

"I regret being in the middle of this, gentlemen, but there appears to be no help for it."

Pete asked, "What can you tell us, Father?"

"Almost nothing I'm afraid, at the moment anyhow. Are you lawmen?"

"We work for the federal government. We want to bring in Matt Moody."

The priest smiled. "Every honest person wants that. He is a scourge."

They showed him their credentials, and the old man nodded. "I will endeavor to get you together with the writer of the note. Of course, he wishes to know what payment he can expect. I assure you, he is a poor man."

Laredo handed over a gold piece. "Give him this then, if you will. When will you see him?"

"Very soon. Perhaps you can return here this evening . . . ?"

They nodded, and Pete said, "We'll be here.

The writer of the note turned out to be a man about Father Julian's age. His name was Andrew Lara, and he was very nervous, saying he was deathly afraid of Moody and his gang. "They are killers, all of them. . . ."

"Nothing you tell us will ever get out," Laredo promised. "The only way Moody will know you told us is if you tell him yourself."

"God forbid!" Lara sat down, shaking his head violently. "I never want to see any of them again!"

"Tell us how you know them," Pete suggested.

"Yes. I have been a school teacher since my college days. My father had a retail business in Illinois with Tom Bowman. I got to know Bowman quite well, as well as his son, Lem. Lem was a peculiar boy, even then."

"In what way?" Laredo asked.

"He liked to take chances, and he ran with a rather wild crowd. I heard my father argue with Mr. Bowman about Lem many times. After I went off to college, they broke up the partnership, and Lem apparently started with the Moody gang. A few years went by, my father died, and I started teaching, and I thought I would never see Lem again. But he showed up at my house one night with another man, needing a place to stay for a few days. The other man was Matt Moody."

"Were they running from the law?"

"Yes. They stayed a week that time—but they paid me well. I had to take the money, to make ends meet."

Laredo asked, "They stayed with you other times?"

"Oh yes, many times over the years. I sold the business after my father died, but I kept the house which was ideally suited to the gang; it was surrounded by an orchard and was not close to other houses. It had a barn and corrals. A dozen men could stay there, and no one would be the wiser. That was a big reason they liked it. And of course I, being a

14

teacher, was very respectable. No one would suspect me of harboring criminals.''

"So you met all the members of the gang?"

"Yes. Matt, Clell, Marty, T.R., and Lem. Lem is the oldest. Matt and T.R. are the quickest with guns, I'd say. Matt likes to drink and was frequently drunk at the house because he was safe there. He's very dangerous when he drinks.'' Lara blinked at them. "What else can I tell you?"

"Did they plan their jobs there?"

"Oh, yes. But they always closed the doors and kept me away. I guess they never really trusted me. I would read in the papers about what they'd done. Usually the jobs were a long way off. I don't think they ever robbed anyone near my house."

"Do you know where Moody is now?"

Lara took a long breath. "I doubt if anyone can be sure. He travels constantly from place to place. He's a very restless man, and he trusts very few. One thing—he worries about the rope, about being hanged."

"Is the gang always together?"

"No, not always. They spend money lavishly when they have it. That's part of the reason they've survived so well. They pay well for information. Bartenders in every town, for instance, keep them informed about the movements of the law. Bartenders hear all sorts of things, you know. I'm surprised no one has ever collected any of the rewards out for them. Maybe, like me, they're afraid to come forward."

Pete asked, "What are your relations with the gang now?"

"I haven't seen any of them for more than a year. They've probably forgotten me, because I sold the house, and they can no longer go there." Lara snapped his fingers. "That reminds me—Lem has a brother who owns a farm near the town of Jewett, about a hundred miles west of here. I heard him mention it once, and I think he and some of the others hid out there as they did at my house."

Laredo nodded. "Very good—what's the brother's name?"

"I think it's Tyron or Tilden—something like that. Last name Bowman, of course."

15

"But he's not a member of the gang?"

"No. He's a farmer. He may not like them any more than I did."

Lara was no longer teaching school. He was getting by tutoring and doing odd jobs and was glad of the money Laredo gave him. He had one other bit of information:

"Moody's mother is still alive. She lives near a little town called Peryton on a farm that Matt bought for her. He sends her money from time to time. He might very well go there to hide out if he needed a place. I doubt if the police know about it."

Laredo said, "You've been a great help to us, Mr. Lara. We thank you."

"I hope you catch them all."

"Amen," said Father Julian.

Matt Moody was feeling poorly. His leg was aching just above the knee where, once long ago, a bullet had bored through, scraping the bone. A doctor had told him it would heal perfectly, and it had, except that now and then it ached for no apparent reason.

It was a very good excuse for carrying whiskey in his saddlebags. He nipped from the bottle whenever the ache came on—and sometimes in between. Good sour mash helped smooth over anything.

He also had a cold and was sniffling and coughing. His mother had fixed him a drink with mint leaves and honey in boiling water, and with that and the whiskey he was feeling very little pain by midday.

But the reservation money was safe. He had taken it, in the heavy canvas sack, down across the south field when it was dark. He had dug a deep hole behind the old shack there and dropped the sack in. No one would ever find it by chance. He had also weighted the blue strongbox and sunk it in the river. No one would ever find it either.

When the hullabaloo about the robbery died down, he would dig up the sack, and they'd divvy up the money and might even go their separate ways for a month or so. None of them was desperate for cash at the moment.

He had left the others at Hayestown and would return there in a few days. They all knew where the money was buried.

His mother's house was small, only four rooms and a porch at either end. There was a square kitchen with a counter · pump, two tiny bedrooms, and a parlor, but it was fine for the old woman, not too much for her to keep up. The belly stove in the parlor heated the entire house nicely. And Sam, the hired Negro man, kept the woodbox filled and did the chores around the place.

No one but his men knew where he was; he had come here without going through Peryton. There was always the reward to think about. Many knew him by sight, and the posters had made much of his cheek birthmark. Some fool might try to backshoot him to collect the money, especially when he happened to be alone.

He was sitting on the porch in the sun, with a bottle down beside the chair, when a rider appeared in the road. Matt drew his Colt and laid it in his lap. The man would have gone on by but he noticed the figure on the porch and paused to shade his eyes with a hand. "Matt! Izzat you, Matt?"

It was Bob Flagg. Matt nodded, and Flagg turned in and got down off his horse. "Never expected to see you here, Matt. You all right?"

"Got a cold is all." He was not particularly fond of Flagg.

The other glanced around. "You here alone?"

Moody nodded. He watched Flagg loop the reins over the hitch rack. Flagg said, grinning, "Give us a chance t'visit."

Mrs. Moody came to the door. "Oh it's you, Bob. Thought I heard voices."

"Howdy, Miz Moody. I was just passin' by."

She smiled and went back into the house.

Flagg leaned on the porch rail and watched Matt take a swig from the bottle. Matt said, "Medicine . . ."

Moody looks a bit more than tipsy, Flagg thought. He's probably been drinking for hours.

·17

Bob made some remarks about the weather holding nicely, and Moody only mumbled.

"Like to ask you something, Matt."

"Whut?"

"Like to join up with you'n the boys."

Moody eyed the other owlishly. "We got all we need, Bob. Can't take nobody else."

"One more won't hurt! Hell, I can do lots of things!"

Moody shook his head. "The boys don't want nobody else. We doin' fine as we is."

Flagg was about to retort when Mrs. Moody came to the door again. "Your tea is ready, Matt. Nice'n hot."

Moody got up awkwardly, grabbed the wall, and stumbled inside, followed by Flagg. He stood swaying in the kitchen, and she gave him the cup of mint tea. He sipped it, made a face, went into the parlor, and sat down, sniffling.

Mrs. Moody rattled pans in the kitchen, and Flagg said, "Dammit, what's wrong with me, Matt? Why won't you have me? I ain't got the goddamn plague."

"Don't go hasslin' me, Bob, dammit. I said no, and that's whut I mean." He gulped the hot tea.

Flagg walked to the window and stared out at the weedy yard. Matt had always acted as if were better and smarter. He was a few years older, that was all.

Matt put the empty cup down and stood up to get a cigar.

Flagg glared at the other's back—and suddenly pulled his pistol. As he yanked back the hammer, Matt heard the *click-clack* and began to turn, eyes wide. But he was not quick enough. Flagg shot him from six feet away and saw him fall.

Then he shoved the gun into his belt and bolted for the front door. Mrs. Moody ran into the parlor and screamed, seeing her son on the floor, his shirt bloody. She grabbed up Matt's pistol and fired wildly from the doorway. As Flagg jumped over the porch railing for his horse, she snapped another shot at him, splintering a roof eave. She ran, slamming the front door open, and emptied the gun in his direction. Her last shot smashed a fence post as Flagg galloped the horse into the road.

18

Then she dropped the pistol and hurried back into the parlor. Matt was alive, lying on his back, looking surprised and scared. She yelled for Sam, who had heard the shots and now ran from the barn, answering her shouts. She told him to hook up the buckboard, toss a tick into the back, and bring it to the back door. He scurried into the barn.

Between them, they carried Matt out to the wagon. The birthmark on his cheek was deep red; his face pasty. Sam drew a blanket over him and tucked it in. Mrs. Moody climbed into the wagon bed and settled herself.

"Go on, get us into town."

She held a compress over the wound as Sam drove.

Dr. Shipley was in. He and Sam carried the wounded man inside and laid him on a table in the office. Mrs. Moody said, "He been shot, Doc."

Shipley arranged the lanterns as his wife shooed them into the hall. "Sit, sit—if you're going to wait."

After about an hour the doctor emerged, his white coat dappled with blood. He clasped both of Mrs. Moody's hands. "He's going to be all right, Clara."

"Oh, thank God!"

"The bullet went in just under the collarbone. I had to fish it out."

"Is he in pain?"

"Not now. I gave him something. He's asleep. I'll give you a bottle of laudanum to take with you when he goes home. He's strong as an ox. He'll be up and around in a few weeks."

"You're going to keep him here?"

"It's best for a few days, yes. I want to watch his progress." Shipley frowned. "Who shot him?"

"Bob Flagg."

"Flagg! Well, I'll be damned! That little weasel! I wouldn't have thought he'd have the nerve—not even to shoot Matt in the back."

She sighed. "Matt was drinking. I guess he thought he could get away with it."

"Well, he didn't do a good enough job. Fortunately for

Matt, the bullet missed the spine." Shipley shook his head. "Or it'd be all over." He patted her hand. "I expect you'll want to keep this secret."

"Yes. yes. Please don't let anyone know."

"All right. You go on home. Leave everything to me. You can see him any time you want."

She nodded and went to the door. "What a terrible thing. Thank you, Doc. I'll come in tomorrow, then." Sam opened the door for her, and she went out.

She had Sam drive at once to the telegraph office. She sent a carefully worded message to Frank Griff in Camp Hill, confident it would reach Marty Nevers.

It did. Marty took the next stage to Peryton.

Chapter Four

WHEN Marty arrived in Peryton, he got a horse at the local livery and hurried at once to Mrs. Moody's home, where he learned that Matt had been shot.

"Who the hell shot him?"

"Bob Flagg."

"That little skunk! Who knows about this, Miz Moody?"

"Not many. Doc Shipley and his wife, me and Sam."

"Who's Sam?"

"The hired man. He won't talk." She scowled. "And of course, Bob Flagg."

"Where's he at?"

She shrugged. "I dunno. I think he lives in a boarding-house in town, but I bet he ain't there now."

"Flagg shot him in the back?"

"Yes, then he run out. I shot at him, but he got away, damn him."

Marty tapped his chin. "So he doesn't know how bad hit Matt is."

"He couldn't."

"So he might think Matt is dead."

She frowned at him. "Don't say that!"

Marty smiled. "It would be better for Matt and all of us if people thought he was dead. The law would stop looking for him."

She stared at him and bit her lip, then slowly nodded. "That's true. They'd leave him be."

"When did the doc say he could be moved?"

"In a day or so."

"Let's go in tomorrow night and get him. He'll be safer here."

Doc Shipley, after talking to Marty Nevers, quickly agreed to announce to the local weekly that Matt Moody had expired as a result of a gunshot wound. Flagg was not mentioned. Shipley gave out no details. Moody had been brought to him, he said, and had died on the operating table. It was all he knew.

Marty arranged for a funeral and burial. He had Sam make a coffin and partially fill it with dirt and rocks, then nail it tight shut. Sam then drove the wagon into town with Mrs. Moody in a heavy veil and Marty on the livery horse.

Sam drove to the cemetery on the edge of town, where a grave digger had the hole ready. Marty had hired a preacher who said appropriate words over the dirt-filled coffin, then it was slowly lowered into the grave as the solemn watchers surrounded it, and Mrs. Moody tossed in a handful of earth.

Matt stayed home in bed with a bottle in one hand and his pistol in the other.

The news that Matt Moody had finally met with a violent end caused a sensation across the land. Laredo and Pete Torres read the account in a local paper and immediately wired John Fleming: Was the story true?

Fleming replied that he did not know. According to the information he had been able to gather, Moody was buried in the town cemetery at Peryton. The best way to find out the truth, Fleming said, was to dig up and open the coffin. He suggested they go at once to Peryton. The government was very interested in the matter and wanted to know if the long chase after Moody *had* come to an end.

However, Fleming reminded them that Moody and his gang had always been full of tricks. They were to believe nothing they could not verify. It was entirely possible Moody had planned and executed his "death."

They took the stage and stepped down at Peryton in a light spring rain. Peryton was a small community, a wide place in the road, only a short stop on the stage line. It had a single, not very straight street, with stores and shacky buildings mostly on the east side, except in the center of town where the only hotel stood, next to the Two Barrels Saloon.

They signed for a room and went first to call on the town undertaker, Mr. Leeds, who was a spare, middle-aged man dressed in traditional black. His undertaking parlor was in a store building, and his office was the size of a cluttered shoe box. They crowded into it, and Laredo asked about Moody.

"Did you bury him, Mr. Leeds?"

"I officiated, yes."

"What does that mean, officiated?"

Leeds looked down his nose at them. "I was there in my official capacity, sir."

"Did you put the body into the coffin?"

The undertaker did not like the question. "What is this all about?"

"We are very curious persons," Laredo told him. "Is the body of Matt Moody in that coffin?"

"Of course it is!"

"Did you see it? Did you actually see the dead body?"

Leeds rose, grasping one lapel. "You have no right to be asking me these questions!"

"I see. You have been paid to say nothing?"

"I resent that, sir!"

Pete said, "You are the obvious person to ask."

Laredo regarded the other steadily. "You really do not know if the body of Matt Moody is in that coffin or not, do you?"

Leeds could see he was outnumbered. "I—I was told . . . it was."

"Who told you?"

Hesitation. "Mr. Smith."

23

"Who is Mr. Smith?"

"I don't know. He and Mrs. Moody brought the coffin to the cemetery. Why would they do that unless he was dead?"

"We can think of a reason," Pete said. "So you took his word for it?"

"I had to. They wouldn't let me—" He paused.

"They wouldn't let you—what?"

Leeds took a long breath. "The coffin was nailed shut. It could not be opened."

Laredo glanced at Pete. "Thank you, Mr. Leeds."

They left the office, and Pete rolled a cigarette in the street. "There's no Matt Moody in that coffin, although they'd like us to think so."

"I wonder if we can dig it up."

"Let's ride out and look at the grave."

The cemetery was on a flat, treeless plain, badly kept up. There had once been a white fence around it, but it was mostly lying flat, overgrown with weeds. All the headboards were wood, many rotted away and lying in pieces. Many were sagging, though a few were fairly new.

But they could find no headboard for Matt Moody.

Laredo said, "They're making sure no one digs up the coffin."

"According to John Fleming, Marty Nevers has used the Smith alias before."

"Let's show Leeds pictures of the gang."

They returned to the hotel, retrieved the pictures, and went to call on Leeds again. He was not happy to see them. He seemed even more defensive.

Laredo took him by the arm and led him into the tiny office. "We only want to show you some photographs."

Pete laid them out on the desk. "Which one is Mr. Smith?"

Leeds sighed, saw that he had no choice, and pointed to the photograph of Nevers.

"You know his real name?"

Leeds sighed again. "Marty Nevers."

"You also know the others?"

Leeds nodded. "I have seen them."

"Is Marty still in town?"

"I have no idea. How would I know?"

"Talk gets around in a small town." Laredo picked up the photos. "Where does Mrs. Moody live?"

"Somewhere out of town."

"Where?"

"I don't know. I've never been there."

"Have you seen any of these men in town lately?"

"No. Only Nevers."

"Thank you, Mr. Leeds."

They returned to the hotel and Pete said, "This entire story about Moody's killing is definitely a hoax. There was a funeral, and a coffin was buried. But there's no headboard and, thanks to the rain, it's impossible to tell which is the most recent grave. The town undertaker did not prepare the body, he admits he never saw the body. . . ." He shrugged. "I think Marty Nevers engineered it all."

"And the local law is probably in Moody's pay—or owes him, so he won't permit us to dig up a grave."

"If we knew which one to dig up."

"Well," Laredo said, "if Moody was shot, the local doctor probably treated him. We can go see him in the morning."

Because of the possibility that the law was in Moody's pay, Laredo and Pete did not introduce themselves. But as they left the restaurant that evening, two men closed in on them, and one leveled a pistol.

"You two are under arrest."

Laredo halted. The two wore silver stars on their vests, with the word "Deputy." He asked mildly, "What's the charge, officers?"

The man with the gun was the larger. He had black hair and a full mustache and thick sideburns. His face was flushed, and his voice grated. "Never mind charges . . ."

The other man was shorter and sallow-faced. He barked, "Turn around, both of you!"

Laredo glanced at Pete. "Certainly." He began to turn, kicked out suddenly, and the pistol went flying. Black Hair yelled, then went to his knees as Laredo's fist hammered him. Pete slugged the other, who fell onto the hitch rack, slid off into the street, and lay gasping.

"That ends our welcome," Laredo said and led the way into the hotel. They went past the round-eyed clerk who had seen it all and out the back door to the stables. They quickly saddled the livery horses and rode down the alley. It was a dark night with no moon.

Halting at the edge of town, Laredo said, "John told us that Moody is considered some kind of a Robin Hood hereabouts. Those deputies probably decided we were asking too many questions."

"I think so," Pete agreed.

"If Moody were really dead, would they care?"

"Probably not. How fast d'you think they can get a posse together?"

"I'd say they'll wait until morning."

Pete grinned. "Then let's go see the doctor tonight."

Two boys playing catch in a dusty street gave them directions to the doctor's house. They left the horses at a hitch rack around the corner from the main street and walked a short distance to the house. Mrs. Shipley opened the door to their knock. "Yes?"

"We'd like to speak to the doctor, please."

She looked them over. "Are you hurt?"

"No."

"What is it you want to talk about? The doctor is very busy at the moment."

"We want to ask him about Matt Moody."

She tried to close the door. "We have nothing to say to you."

Laredo easily pushed the door open and stepped into a hall. "Where is the doctor?"

She was suddenly angry, and her voice turned shrill. "You must leave at once! You can't push in here like this!"

Shipley came from his office. He was wearing a white coat and took off his glasses. "What's going on here?"

Laredo said, "We'd like to talk to you about Matt Moody, Doctor."

"I heard my wife just tell you—"

"We're sorry to push in this way—but it's important."

"Who are you?"

Laredo took out his credentials and passed them over. "We work for the government as investigators. Did you treat Matt Moody recently for gunshot wounds?"

Pete closed the door behind them. Mrs. Shipley looked apprehensive. The doctor handed back the papers and sighed.

"Yes, I treated him."

"Please go on."

Shipley shrugged. "I simply treated him and sent him away."

"Then he is alive?"

"Yes, certainly he is."

Pete said sharply: "Horses outside. I think we have company." He bolted the door.

Laredo said, "We don't want to cause you trouble. Please tell them you told us nothing." He hurried down the hall. "We'll go out this way."

They found themselves in a kitchen and opened the back door to a porch. Laredo stepped down to the grass as a horseman came around the house. The man saw them and fired too quickly. Pete sent a shot after him, and the man swore.

They ran past the stable into an alleyway. Suddenly, men were shouting as they sprinted toward the main street in the dark. Someone fired at them from the stable, but the bullets went wide. They were only shadows in the night. But the horsemen were coming, the galloping horses sounding louder and louder. . . .

Then Laredo turned into an alcove, squeezing past a fence and a wall. Pete followed, and they came into a cluttered yard as the mounted men streamed past.

They were between two houses that faced a lane. Across the lane were dark fields. Along the narrow little street were

27

more houses with lights coming on as people heard the commotion.

Pete said, "We can't stay here." He ran into the field, and Laredo hurried after, looking back over his shoulder.

Apparently, the two deputies had gotten a posse together very quickly. And one of them had been smart enough to think about Dr. Shipley. If they hadn't made so much noise . . .

Pete swore, almost stumbling into a ditch. He caught himself and motioned, "Get down."

Shadowy figures appeared along the lane, and they could hear voices.

Pete said, "Let's follow this ditch."

"Lead on."

The arroyo seemed to parallel the distant lane. They had gone only a few hundred yards when horsemen came galloping into the fields, calling to each other. But none came near.

They moved away from the pursuers and went back to the lane and to the street where they'd left the horses. As they rode out of town Laredo commented, "John will be interested to learn Moody is alive. But we can't wire him from here."

"Moody's probably staying at his mother's farm. If we knew where it is."

"I wonder who shot him. You don't suppose it was Marty Nevers?"

"Trying to become gang leader?"

"Maybe."

"Undertaker Leeds told us that Marty came into town with Moody's mother and the coffin. Would she be friendly with Nevers if he had shot her son?"

"Not likely. Unless it was an accident."

"It's hard to believe he was shot by accident."

Laredo nodded. "He must have a lot of enemies."

Chapter Five

THE news of Clell's death had been kept out of the papers, but word came to Marty Nevers in Peryton, and he discussed it with Matt at once.

"They say a couple of detectives came to Hayestown looking for Clell. One said he was a cousin."

Matt said, "Clell didn't have no cousin. He didn't have no folks at all."

"Yeh. That's how they knew it was a lie. Clell set a trap for them but got caught in it hisself."

Matt sighed deeply. Damn. Clell, he was a good man. "You find out who them detectives were?"

"No. Maybe Pinkertons."

"And they got away clear?"

"Yeah. Afraid so." Marty paused. "You hurtin' much?"

Matt shifted uncomfortably. "Course it hurts. That son of a bitch, Bob Flagg. I'm gonna shoot his ass off when I get outa here."

"He ain't in town. I looked for him."

Matt growled. "You leave him be. He's mine. I'll fix 'is goddamn wagon." He groaned. "Hand me that bottle."

When he heard the two detectives were in Peryton asking questions, Marty wired the others to come at once. Matt might be in danger. The best and quickest way to get rid of the danger would be to get rid of the detectives.

With descriptions from the saloon girl, Cora, from Undertaker Leeds, and Dr. Shipley, they had a good picture of the two: a young blondish man and a big Mexican.

When T.R. and Lem arrived, they combed the town for them and turned up nothing.

"They got out," Marty told Matt. "Maybe heard we was looking for them."

There were a good many farms and isolated houses surrounding Peryton. It might take months to investigate them all—in the careful manner they had to follow. It would certainly be exceedingly foolish and dangerous to go riding up to Moody's house in daylight.

"He'll shoot on sight," Pete said. "They know what we look like by now."

The next town on the telegraph was a railroad spur named Hanover. They made the journey and reported to John Fleming that Matt Moody definitely was not dead and was probably recovering at his mother's farm near Peryton. And the others of the gang could be with him.

Fleming wired back definite instructions. They were not, under *any* circumstances, to attempt to round up Moody and the gang. It would probably be suicide for two men to try. He was contacting the War Department, requesting a troop of cavalry to surround the house. He asked them to remain in Hanover. He would wire them when the gang was rounded up and in jail.

Orders were orders. They took a room at the hotel and whiled away the time. If the army was successful, then their job was at an end.

Fleming's next wire was five days in coming. The cavalry had sent a troop of fifty men and . . . they had let the gang slip through their fingers. Fleming's wire was brief, but it was easy to read his disgust in the words. The army had been clumsy and stupid.

The search for Moody was on again.

"If we go back to Peryton," Laredo said, "we may be able to pick up some threads."

30

"If the troopers haven't trampled them all out. I'll bet it was one of Fleming's superiors who decided to use the cavalry."

"No bet."

They returned to Peryton at once, but there was nothing to find. They were directed to the Moody farm, but Mrs. Moody had nothing to say to them. She slammed the door in their faces.

A boy from town, who helped Sam with the farm chores, brought news of the cavalry. The boy told Sam that Mr. Sidden, the grocer, had said it was the first time he had ever seen troopers in town.

Sam thought it curious enough to mention to Marty Nevers.

Marty never hesitated. He ordered Sam to hook up the buckboard. He and T.R. carried Matt out and put him in the wagon bed on a mattress. Lem packed a gunnysack with food, and they hurried away from the farm, all inside of fifteen minutes.

The cavalry arrived an hour later, sabers rattling.

Marty left T.R. behind to watch the place. "Stay out of sight." Toby was able to report later that the cavalry had indeed surrounded the house. Mrs. Moody had come out and asked them what they wanted.

It was Marty's guess that Bob Flagg had told the government where Matt was to be found. It was another nail in Flagg's coffin.

They were two hours along the road when Marty asked, "Where do we go? We got to hide out where we can get to a doc."

"My brother's place," Lem offered. "They don't know about him."

"Good," Marty said. They set a course for Jewett.

They stopped every hour or so to rest Matt. The buckboard had no springs, and the road was nothing but ruts. It was an ordeal for a wounded man.

31

On one of the halts Matt said he had been thinking. Why didn't they go on to Mexico? "We'd be safe there."

"You can't make it," Marty objected. "This goddamn wagon is poundin' you as it is. Mexico's too far."

"I can handle it."

"No, you can't."

Lem and Toby agreed with Marty. T.R. said, "That wound'll open up, and you'll bleed to death. Besides, like Marty says, we got to get you to a doc ever' now 'n' then to make sure you're healin' right."

Matt sighed and lay back. He was weak as a horned toad and gave up arguing. He had a long drink from the bottle before they went on. It was the only thing that smoothed out the bumps.

It took nearly four days to get to Jewett, a town about the size of Peryton. They convinced Matt to see the local doctor at once. Dr. Clavin was an old man, stooped and fussy. He seldom went out of the house. Patients came to him, or they died somewhere else. He peered at Matt, poked and sniffed, rubbed him with carbolic acid, rebandaged him; and asked for three dollars.

Clavin's male nurse, a skinny man of thirty-five with thick glasses, said, "We ought to change that bandage in three or four days."

Marty asked, "Why d'you have to do that?"

"Because the wound's got to drain. There'll be trouble if it doesn't."

"Can you do that"—Marty motioned—"without the old man?"

"Sure. Where you going to be?"

"Out to the Bowman place. You know where it is?"

"Yeh, I know."

Marty slipped him a five-dollar gold piece. "Come out then, in a few days. But keep it to yourself."

The skinny man smiled. "I will."

The Bowman farm was a bit more than five miles from town in a wide, shallow valley graced by a large, weedy pond. Tyler Bowman was a big, thickset man who looked nothing at all like Lem, his more slender brother. He was also older and getting gray. He seemed glad to see Lem but frowned at the others.

"Who you got in the wagon?"

"He's a friend. He been shot. You mind if we put up in the barn for a spell? We won't be no trouble to you."

"How long you fixin' to stay?"

"Maybe a week . . ."

The big farmer sighed. "You still runnin' from the law, Lem? Did you bring 'em here?"

"Nobody's chasin' us, Ty."

Tyler sighed again and nodded. His attitude was defensive, as if he had little choice. His visitors were all heavily armed and might be touchy. His wife stood in the back door of the house, staring at the newcomers, obviously no more happy to see them than her husband was.

It was a large barn and had a room built on behind, as a bunkhouse, used at harvest time by field hands. It contained six built-in bunk beds and was currently unoccupied. They carried Matt in and made him comfortable in one of the lowers. There was a big iron stove in the middle of the room. It had a flat area used for cooking, and that evening, as they made a stew in a pot, T.R. asked about money.

Marty looked at him. "You broke again?"

"Stony broke. We shoulda grabbed some of that reservation money before we left."

Marty nodded. "There wasn't no time. And we can't go back right now."

T.R. grinned. "Where's the nearest bank?"

"I seen one in Jewett."

"Too close to home," Lem said.

Toby made a face. "That's why they'll never look here."

"That could be," Marty agreed. "Sheriffs got no imagination."

"Five minutes in and out and we got all the cash we need," T.R. said. "We ride out north and circle around when it gets dark. Hell, they'll never find us."

"We that desperate for cash?" Lem asked.

"Toby is. I got some left," Marty said, "but we got to pay your brother something, and we got to pay the doc."

"Who's goin' with me?" Toby asked.

"I will," Marty said. He pointed to Lem. "You stay with Matt. Me and Toby will bring back the bacon. It shouldn't take more'n two to crack that little bank. What day is it?"

"Tuesday."

T.R. said, "When you want to do it?"

"We ought to ride in and look over the town first. We could do that at night, maybe tomorrow. All right?"

T.R. nodded.

"Don't bring nobody back here," Lem said, growling.

"We won't," Toby assured him. "We'll be in and out of that bank in some minutes. I bet they don't even chase us."

Lem asked, "Where we going to take Matt from here?"

Marty looked at the hurt man in the bunk; he was snoring lightly. "What about Velma. Remember her?"

"Saloon in Hatcher!" T.R. said, "Yeah, I sure do. We could put Matt in one of the upstairs rooms. And the law's cheap there. Just a town marshal."

Marty nodded. "We can go soon's we get us some kale."

Marty and T.R. walked their horses along the main street of the town shortly before midnight. The only bank, the Jewett Bank & Trust, was in the center of town on a corner. The side street ran east and west; the eastern end petered out in a field. Across the wide, brushy expanse was a straggly wood on a slope. There were no fences.

As they rode back to the farm it began to rain lightly. By the time they reached the barn they were both swearing—it was a downpour, hammering the grass flat, soaking them to the skin.

They wiped down the horses, then stripped and stood by the fire. Marty growled, saying they would have to put off the bank job. The ground would be mud, and they would leave tracks that a cigar-store Indian could follow with half an eye.

The storm had passed by morning, and a halfhearted sun

came out but grew stronger as the day progressed. Matt was groaning and feeling uncomfortable, though his cold had about disappeared. T.R. rode into town and returned with the skinny assistant in a light buggy.

His name was Dan, he told them, and he'd had medical training. He had a bag and a bundle of bandages. He gently and deftly removed Matt's stained dressings and clucked his tongue. The wound was red and warm to the touch. He treated it with carbolic acid and rebandaged it. "That's all that can be done."

Out of Matt's hearing, he indicated the whiskey bottle. "Let him have all that he wants. It'll ease the discomfort."

Marty walked out to the buggy with him and gave him another five-dollar gold piece. "Thanks for comin'. But keep this visit under your hat."

Dan nodded and drove back to town.

They strolled into the bank in the afternoon just before closing time. There were three customers at the windows, and Toby herded them and the tellers into a corner. "Don't do nothing foolish, gents." They looked at the muzzle of his revolver and shook their heads.

Marty gathered up the cash in the till boxes and drawers, stuffing it into a canvas sack. The big safe was already locked for the day, one of the tellers told them.

It was a small bank, employing only two tellers. There were also two bank officers, one of them the owner, according to the sign on his office door. The officers were both older men. They stood with their hands in the air, watching Marty fill the sack. Both were pale and nervous.

When he had all the cash, Marty said, "All right. Let's go."

T.R. went out first and swung into the saddle. The street was empty of traffic; the town dozed in the late sun. Marty ran out and climbed on his horse as one of the bank officers appeared in the doorway with a shotgun. He fired too fast. The buckshot whined over their heads, and T.R. cut the man

35

down, firing three times with his six-gun. The banker crumpled on the steps and slid facedown into the dirt.

Marty and T.R. galloped the horses along the side street toward the fields. The job had taken only a few minutes.

Several men ran into the street behind them and fired pistols without result. With T.R. in the lead they galloped across the near field and into the woods. At the ridge they halted and looked back. No one was coming after them.

"Take 'em a while to get organized," Marty said.

They made a wide circle, east then south, looking for hard ground to hide their tracks. Far to the south they followed a meandering road that led generally west. They left it in a wash and cut across country to the Bowman farm, arriving after dusk.

When they counted the money on a table in the barn, they had six thousand and forty-three dollars.

Chapter Six

Andrew Lara had told them about Lem's brother's farm near Jewett. Of course, as Pete said, the gang could have gone anywhere from Peryton, but Jewett seemed a good bet. They might have many friends or people like themselves who would hide them out, but the Bowman farm was the best possibility *they* knew, Laredo agreed, and Pete said they should check it out.

It was certain that Matt Moody would have to receive constant medical attention—for a while at least. So when they arrived in Jewett, their first stop was to see the only doctor in town. His name was Clavin, and he was old and infirm. He seldom left the office he told them, and yes, he had treated a man with a gunshot wound very recently. He treated dozens every year.

But he did not know the name Moody.

Clavin's assistant was a skinny man with thick glasses. He listened to the conversation then followed them out to the horses. "The doctor did not treat a gunshot wound lately," he said. "His memory's not so good anymore, but he won't admit it."

Laredo asked, "Is there another doctor anywhere near?"

"No, not within a couple day's ride."

Laredo thanked the assistant, and he and Pete mounted and rode into the center of town. "Who do you believe, the doctor or the assistant?"

Pete rolled a cigarette and fished for a match. "We know that Moody and his gang have paid off bartenders and lawmen for years. Why not a doctor's assistant? He seemed a slippery sort."

"Yes. He might lead us to Moody."

They took a room in the Jewett Hotel and watched the doctor's house. They followed the assistant here and there, but he did not lead them out of town. He patronized several saloons after his day was done, as well as several of the girls, but he definitely did not visit Matt Moody.

Neither did Dr. Clavin.

"Moody's not in town. We'll have to locate the Bowman farm."

They wired Fleming to let him know where they were.

The same day they wired Fleming they followed the assistant—they had learned his name was Dan—from the Paradise Saloon. Dan was walking unsteadily, and it was very late. The street was deserted as Laredo and Pete each took an arm and led Dan, protesting, around behind the buildings and tossed him into a borrowed wagon. Pete climbed in with him and stifled his yammering.

Laredo drove the one-horse wagon out of town. West of the town was a hilly section with trees and tall brush and a number of sandy washes. He turned into one, several miles from the outskirts, and halted under the lee of a sand cliff.

"A good place for a fire," Laredo said, rubbing his hands together. He quickly gathered several armfuls of dry wood, breaking the sticks into short lengths. Pete lifted Dan out of the wagon.

The assistant had sobered completely. "What d'you two want?"

"Information," Pete said in surprise. "We don't believe your story about Matt Moody."

Dan watched Laredo scoop a hole in the sand and make a little pyramid of dry twigs. When he struck a match, Dan asked, "What we need a fire for?"

Pete said, "It'll help with the questioning."

"I don't know nothing about Matt Moody!"

Laredo said, "Take your shoes off."

Dan stared at him. "What—why?"

Pete said reasonably, "How can we put your feet in the fire with shoes on?"

"What the hell!" Dan was startled.

Pete said, "Of course, we don't *have* to burn you. Tell us what you know about Moody."

The assistant looked at them with a horrified expression on his sallow face. He stared at the yellow flames, and Laredo said, "Well . . . ?"

Pete remarked, "We can take the shoes off for you."

Dan wilted. He sighed deeply and closed his eyes. "I rode out to the Bowman place and rebandaged Moody. Dr. Clavin doesn't know about it."

"How is Moody?"

"He'll recover. He was shot in the back. The bullet lodged under the clavicle—the collarbone. Somebody already took it out. Now the wound is draining."

"You say he'll recover?"

"Oh yes."

"You're not a doctor."

Dan shrugged. "I've dealt with hundreds of gunshots. I can do it as well as Clavin."

"Who was with Moody?"

"Three men, and of course the Bowmans, Tyler and his wife. They're not in the house. They had Moody in a room behind the barn."

"And they paid you to keep your mouth shut?"

Dan nodded.

"Are they still at the farm?"

"As far's I know. They were there the last time I saw them. I've told you everything I know."

Pete said, "Except one thing. Where's the farm?"

Dan gave them directions, and Laredo covered the fire with sand. They drove back into town, let Dan go, and returned the wagon.

In the hotel room Pete asked, "Are they still at the Bowman farm?"

"We ought to go look."

"What about the cavalry?"

Laredo laughed. "We shouldn't allow the army to embarrass itself again."

They were in a saloon the next afternoon, at the far end of town, whiling away the time until dark, when they planned to visit the Bowman farm. Suddenly they heard shots. No one in the saloon budged; gunfire was not that uncommon. A few men looked around, and that was all.

But five or six minutes later a man came into the saloon to say the bank had just been robbed. "There was two of them, and they got away clean."

Someone asked, "Where's the deputy?"

No one had seen him.

One man, the bank owner, had been killed, the informant said. "He run out with a shotgun, and they bunged him up."

Laredo said softly to Pete, "Would they rob the bank here?"

"I wouldn't put anything past them."

"Of course, it could be another bunch."

"It could be."

They rode to the Bowman place that night, approaching it well after dark. There was a house, a long adobe outbuilding, and a corral by the barn. On foot, Laredo went close; the house was dark, and there was no one in the barn and only one lonely mule in the corral.

The birds had flown.

There was no good reason to ride back into town; they had left nothing there. They rolled their blankets in the barn. In the morning, when he came out of the house, Tyler Bowman was astonished to see them.

"What you all doin' here?"

Laredo said, "Looking for Matt Moody."

Bowman hung onto his suspender straps and stared at both of them. "Moody ain't here." His voice was unfriendly. "If you ain't the law, you better git."

40

"Moody *was* here. Where did he and the others go?"

"How the hell do I know? I ought t'charge you all for feed for your horses."

Laredo handed him four bits. "You didn't talk to them at all."

Bowman growled and put the coin in his pocket. "They didn't tell me nothing—and I don't want t'know."

They mounted and rode out.

"Bowman probably didn't know," Laredo said when they were alone. "The gang would never tell him, an outsider."

But the wheels of the buckboard left a plain trail.

Chapter Seven

HATCHER was a sprawling town on the edge of a long strip of badlands. On the other side was desert that turned into prairie several days' ride north. Near the town was a small river that had been tamed in part by the erection of a heavy earthen dam, which formed a small lake. A tunnel through the dam allowed the river water to continue.

It was cow country to the south, and Hatcher served half a dozen ranches, some nesters, and a few farmers. The town had a red-light district to rival the big railroad towns to the north, a dozen saloons and deadfalls.

One of the saloon/dance halls, the Red Slipper, was owned by Velma Kopin. Her husband had died and left her everything—they had no children—and she managed it better than he had.

It was an unhappy day, she said, when they brought Matt Moody to her establishment in the buckboard. She ordered him carried upstairs to rooms near her own, above the dance hall, and put to bed. Then she sent someone for Dr. Weaver.

"Who the hell shot 'im?"

"A sneaky little jasper named Bob Flagg."

She turned in surprise. "Was he alone? What happened to Flagg?"

Marty shrugged. "We ain't found Flagg yet, but he'll turn up dead one o' these days. Matt was at his mother's house. She says Flagg come in and they was arguin'."

"And Matt turned his back."

"Must have."

Doc Weaver was a middle-aged man, short and grizzled, wearing thick glasses. Velma treated him as an old friend, sliding her arm about his shoulders. "You was never here, Doc. You never saw this patient."

"Of course not, Velma."

"No matter who asks."

"I got you. Now lemme look at him." He shooed them out and examined Matt, rebandaged him, and ordered that he not be moved.

"He needs a lot of rest. Let him be right where he is. I'll come back tomorrow."

Velma went to the door with him. "Tell Charlie downstairs to give you anything you want."

He nodded and went down the steps.

Velma had plenty of room for them. Her own apartment was at the back of the building, closed off from the others and could be reached only by an outside stairway. She put Marty, Lem, and T.R. into two of the spare rooms next to a storeroom. Matt was in a room by himself across the hall.

Velma was a big, red-haired woman with a quick mind. She had kept her own books since Harry died, because she was faster at arithmetic than any of the accountants her husband had hired—and more accurate. She knew to a penny what her bar should take in and her bouncer, an ex-pugilist named Dick Jarman, took bartenders aside and talked earnestly to them when differences showed up. He never had to talk to one of them twice.

Her establishment was in three sections: the saloon in the center, the dance hall on the left, and a restaurant on the right. With her keen attention to business and a head for figures, she had become a prosperous woman, a force in the town.

Marty sat with her in one of the restaurant booths while they had breakfast. "You don't look a day older'n the last time we was here, Velma."

43

She chuckled. "I think you said the same thing that time, too. How long you figgerin' to stay?"

"Like to hang around till Matt is well enough to get on a horse."

"That'll be a month at least."

"I guess so. You mind us bein' here?"

"No, of course not!"

"We got money. We'll pay our way."

She sniffed. "Did I mention money?"

Marty smiled. "Money will keep us friends if we pay our keep. We want it that way."

"All right." She smiled back. "And you want Matt's bein' here kept secret."

"Of course. We let it out that he's dead."

"Is anybody on your trail?"

"No."

"Somebody's always on Matt's trail."

"Yeah, maybe, but nobody knows we's here." He laid two gold eagles on the table between them. "This's for a start."

Velma nodded and picked them up. "What handle you using now?"

He thought for a moment. "Call us brothers, if anybody wants to know. We'll be the Harris brothers—Al, Bob, and Cass. You can remember that; A,B,C. Al, Bob, Cass."

She laughed. "Pretty cute; A,B, and C. Which one are you?"

"I'm Al. We done this before. T.R. is Bob, and Lem is Cass."

Doc Weaver was back the next day as promised. He stayed with Matt for half an hour and was guardedly optimistic when he came out of the room.

"He's a strong man, and he's coming round better than I thought he would when I saw him yesterday. The wound is healing nicely, and he's more comfortable." He snapped his bag shut. "I'll see him tomorrow."

Marty walked down to the street with him, receiving a promise to keep Matt's presence under his hat.

T.R. was well satisfied with Velma's saloon. There were five girls working the floor from the middle of the afternoon on. One of them was a honey blonde named Hester. She was very rounded and willing, when she realized he had money, and he monopolized her services.

It was a situation that provoked jealousy in the minds of several who apparently forgot she was for hire. One of these was a man named Dirk Benson—who obviously regarded Hester as something she was not.

Benson quickly learned that T.R. had come between him and the saloon girl of his choice, and he asked one of the bartenders, "Who is this hombre anyhow?"

"I wouldn't fool with him if I was you, D.B. He got two brothers who is loaded for bear."

"Two brothers?"

"One of 'em's sitting right over there now, feller with the cigar." The barman indicated Marty Nevers, who was at a card table with several others.

"Who's the other brother?"

The bartender looked over the saloon. "Don't see 'im."

Benson sipped his beer and thought about it. He was not a gunman, and the bartender had hinted that the brothers were. And T.R., what he had seen of him, looked very fast and capable and wore a pistol under his coat.

It meant he had two choices: Forget it, or do something about T.R. when no one was looking.

He considered the latter choice. He was pretty good with a rifle. He might center T.R. from a distance, and no one could prove he'd done it. The law in Hatcher was a joke, as everyone knew. The marshal was an older man who was often drunk because the saloon keepers fed him free whiskey. Velma and the other merchants paid his meager salary, and he did exactly as they told him.

Benson finished his beer and went outside to look for a place to shoot from.

The bartender, Jonas Neal, watched Benson leave the saloon, and when T.R. came downstairs later, Jonas beckoned

45

to him and leaned over the bar, telling him about Benson. He knew T.R. to be a close friend of his boss.

"If I was you," he said. "I'd watch my back."

"Thanks," T.R. said. "Point him out to me when he comes in again." He slid a greenback into Neal's hand.

The bartender pointed Benson out that evening. T.R. had a notion to go to Lem, and perhaps the two of them could do a bit of persuading, but then why bother Lem? He would take care of this bird himself.

Benson had no idea that T.R. knew he existed, and so T.R. had no trouble discovering what he was about. Hester told him Benson was jealous, so it tallied with what the barman had told him. T.R. was amused that a man would go to all that trouble over a saloon doxie, but Benson was serious.

Earlier in the day Benson had found a niche between two buildings, and now he left the bar and headed there, then climbed into it with a rifle. He had a horse tied in the alley behind the niche.

T.R. let the other man wait several hours, then went around behind the niche and climbed up on a privy to see Benson lying there with the rifle poked out, ready to fire. T.R. yelled, "Hey!"

Benson looked over his shoulder in astonishment, and T.R. shot him twice. Once in the forehead and once in the crotch. Then he went back into the saloon and upstairs to see Hester.

Someone noticed Benson's horse the next day, and a store-keeper found the body. The marshal decided Benson had been feuding with someone unknown and had got the worst of it. There was enough money in the pockets of the body to pay the undertaker, but no one attended the funeral.

However, a reporter for the weekly, a man who also frequented the upstairs brothel, heard the story from the girls. A man had been jealous enough to try to shoot someone else over a cyprian's affections. The girls thought that was funny as hell, and the reporter printed the story, using no names

46

except the victim's and that of the saloon, the Red Slipper. He also printed the odd position of one of the two bullets.

Because of the crotch shot the story was reprinted and eventually found its way into the hands of a sheriff, who declared in a follow-up story that the shooter probably had been Toby Rogers, who ran with the outlaw Matt Moody. Toby, called T.R., had done exactly the same thing before in his county over a saloon girl.

Laredo wired the particulars to John Fleming, saying he and Pete were leaving at once for Hatcher.

Fleming wired them that his superiors were very interested in recovering the one hundred and fifty thousand dollars sent to the Indian agent. They suggested to Fleming that he and his men concentrate on that. Fleming also said that none of the money, the serial numbers of which had been noted, had turned up. The gang had apparently stashed it somewhere to be spent later.

If one of the gang can be captured, Fleming wired them, then there are ways he could be induced to discuss the hiding place.

Matt began to recover rapidly. A week after arriving at Velma's saloon, he was sitting up and even moving about gingerly from the bed to a chair, though it tired him. Doc Weaver saw him daily, changed the bandages regularly, and pronounced him his best patient in years.

Matt talked constantly about going back to find Bob Flagg. The subject never seemed to leave his mind. Even when his visitors discussed other topics, Velma could see he still brooded about Flagg. She said it was probably the hope of shooting Flagg that had hastened Matt's recovery.

Unfortunately, as he recovered he began to drink. He trusted Velma, feeling safe in her house, and the whiskey made the enforced inactivity bearable. He was not a reader and had little interest in newspapers unless an item concerned himself, so he did not read about T.R.'s shooting of Benson, and no one mentioned it to him. When he was drinking he had a too-quick temper. Velma was the only one he did not shout at.

Marty, Lem and T.R. felt the inactivity also, though Lem was more content to play cards in the saloon and while away an hour or two with the girls.

T.R. spent much time with Hester, even taking her on picnics outside the town.

Marty had been talking to some businessmen in saloons, and he discovered there were a surprising number of merchants who did not deal with the small local bank. They preferred to send their funds to Chandler, where they got a better rate of interest. Chandler was about eighty miles to the east, and the money went by special messenger, not the stage.

Marty gleaned these facts over a period of time, and he discussed them with T.R. late at night.

T.R. asked, "What do they mean by special messenger?"

"A man on a horse. Remember the Pony Express back before the war? It's the same idea. The rider is fast and secret. He leaves here at odd times, never on a schedule so no one can predict him. And he carries large amounts of cash for the bank at Chandler."

"Cash?" T.R. smiled. "How much?"

"I don't know. But from what I can learn it's always a lot. They don't send him unless it's plenty. He goes about once a week."

Toby grinned. "So we intercept him."

"Why not?" Marty rubbed his hands together. "We shoot the horse and put him afoot, then we count the cash. We get him in a cross fire. He won't have a chance."

"Hmmm." T.R. frowned. "We can only do it once, huh? Won't they get another system?"

"I guess so. Or keep the secret better. As it is we may not have an easy time finding out when the messenger goes—and they change the route all the time."

"How *do* we find out? Is Velma's money in it?"

"No. There's a few who don't trust banks, and Velma is

one of them." He chuckled. "She knows too many bank robbers."

T.R. scratched his chin. "If we can't find out . . . we can't do nothing."

Marty leaned forward and lowered his voice. "I got an ace in the hole. I know who the messenger is."

"Jesus!" T.R. grinned broadly. "You helt that back long enough! Who is he?"

"Hombre named Johnson. He works at the livery. One of the gents I play cards with let it slip one night. I let 'em think I didn't notice it. I figger if he works at the stable, he got his pick of fast horses. He prob'ly leaves from there, too."

"That's more like it," T.R. said. "Let's get us a map that shows Chandler. How many routes can there be?"

"I think Velma got one in her office. I'll ask her in the morning." Marty tapped his cheek. "Chandler's eighty miles, give or take a few, so the messenger'll have to change horses at least once. They prob'ly got that arranged, too."

"Yeh. A line shack and a corral somewhere."

Marty nodded. "They been doing this for a while. They could be a little careless by now."

"That's a damn shame!" T.R. said, and they both laughed.

Chapter Eight

Bob Flagg felt secure. None of the Moody gang had come after him; he was sure they had no idea where he was. And it would take them a while to learn what had happened to Matt. Maybe, with Matt gone, they had all scattered and weren't even a gang anymore. Flagg was sure Matt was dead. He'd seen Matt fall with the bullet stain on his shirt—he'd probably been hit in the spine and had been dead before he hit the floor. It was too goddamn bad he hadn't been able to stay a minute—but the old woman and her wild shooting could have killed him!

From her house he had gone straight east to Larksburg, where he had friends. All the way he had thought about the reward on Matt, but he'd have had to stay in Peryton to collect it, and no telling when Marty or T.R. would show up.

But he and some of his friends had run off a few cows, sold them, and raised a little hell with the money afterward. He had ideas of doing the same thing again—it had been easy.

Then he had run into Howie Edwards in a saloon. He and Howie had been close buddies—they'd even been in jail together. Howie hadn't changed one whit. He was still skinny, black-haired, and ugly—and still down on his luck.

"Things is bad," he told Flagg. "Since I seen you I spent a year in the county pen. They said I stole a wagon."

"Did you?"

"Sure." Howie grinned, then sighed. "A goddamn bad-luck wagon. I never even got to sell 'er."

"You broke?"

"No, I got maybe a dollar."

Flagg laughed. "I can spare you ten."

Howie brightened a little. "Let's you'n me go over to Corona or one of them big towns and get into the holdup business."

Flagg pulled at his chin. "We can have a drink and talk about it."

"All right."

There was a line of posters near the saloon door, and one of them proclaimed in big black letters: WANTED for Murder MATT MOODY. It gave particulars. Flagg tapped the poster. "They can take that one down. Matt's dead."

"I heard he was. Thought it was newspaper talk."

"Hell no. I shot 'im."

Howie was astonished. "You shot Matt Moody?"

"Yeh, I did. He pulled a gun on me, and he was slow. Nothing to it. He got a big reputation and nothing to back it up."

They sat at a table with beer in front of them. Howie said, "I never knew you was a slick gun-hand, Bob."

Flagg made a face. "I never claimed to be no Bill-show expert, but I wasn't afraid of Matt Moody neither."

"None of the gang around?"

"Didn't happen to be."

"How come you shot him?"

"We was talkin' about me joining up with him and the rest. I tole him I didn't want to join, and he got kind of nasty about it. He been drinking of course, and Matt gets mean when he drinks. He called me some names when I wouldn't join, and then all of a sudden he yanks out his gun!" Flagg shrugged. "So I had to shoot 'im."

"Well, I be damned."

"He didn't leave me no choice. I didn't want to hang around till the rest of 'em showed up. You know what hot-heads they is—prob'ly shoot before I could explain."

"They would, too," Howie agreed. He sipped the beer. "What about Corona?"

"It don't sound too bad. You want to take a bank, or what?"

"Well, we can look the town over, see what we think. But I'd rather take a stage than a bank."

"All right. Let's look it over."

Laredo and Pete took the stagecoach to Hatcher, a larger town than they'd supposed. There were a dozen saloons and dance halls in the town, and on weekends the place was alive with people, lights, laughter, and gunshots. Cowhands would come galloping into town shooting off six-guns for the hell of it. They flocked into the saloons to see the girlie shows; the streets were full of drunks. Everything was for sale.

But the Moody gang was not in evidence. With the pictures of the gang firmly in mind, Laredo and Pete separated and nosed through every saloon and hall, coming up empty.

There were two doctors in town, one named Weaver, the other Durwent. They visited both, and neither had ever seen Matt Moody, they said, nor treated him.

"We may have lost him," Laredo said gloomily.

"The trail led this way."

"But not to their door. Do you suppose the doctors are lying to us?"

Pete took off his hat and scratched his head. "It's possible. Moody can offer more bribes than us. But maybe he's well enough now not to need a doctor's services."

"I was afraid you'd say that."

Pete put the hat back on. "You know what I've been wondering?"

"What?"

"Why the gang is still together. Dr. Clavin's assistant told us they were. But they have one hundred and fifty thousand dollars in their possession. Why haven't they split it up and gone to spend it? We know they have in the past."

"It's possible they know the numbers have been listed, and they've cached it for the time being."

Pete nodded. "Yes. It's the only explanation I can think of, too."

"And the reason they're all staying together is that they all know where the money is."

Pete smiled. "So they don't trust each other?"

"One hundred and fifty thousand is a lot of trust—for crooks like them." Laredo sighed. "Of course we both could be wrong, and the reason we can't find them is that they *have* split up the money and are all on the way to St. Louis for a big blowout."

"Would they leave Moody to do that?"

"Let's hope not . . . because if they did, the money's gone."

Pete said, "Shall we try the town marshal?"

"I'm afraid we have to. He's our last lead."

The law in Hatcher was named Bill Symes. He was employed by the town council to keep order. He had a tiny office and four cells in a brick building. He received two dollars for every drunk he locked up. It was his only source of income. His clothes were seedy, and he was unshaven—a stranger could not have picked him out of a lineup with his inmates. But he was sober. He was nodding behind a battered desk, his feet up on an opened drawer, when they entered. Someone in a jail cell was singing a mourning song about a girl who had left him.

Pete shook Symes awake, and they showed him their credentials. "We're looking for Matt Moody."

Symes yawned. "Don't know a thing about Moody, gents. Not a thing."

"He's not in town?" Laredo asked.

"If he is, I don't know it." Symes was a bloated wretch, probably in his fifties. His broad face was blotchy, and his hands trembled; he seldom met their eyes. He fiddled with a watch chain and scratched his belly.

There was nothing to be gained here. Laredo glanced at Pete who shook his head, and they thanked the man and left. On the street Laredo said, "Will he go straight to Moody to tell him about us?"

"Yes, or send someone. I wouldn't trust him with half a frog." Pete rolled a brown cigarette. "Why don't we watch his door?"

Farther down the street from the marshal's office was an abandoned shack. It had only three sides and part of a roof, but from it they were able to keep a watch on the office door. Hours went by, and Symes did not appear.

Pete said, "Maybe Moody isn't in town after all."

"Or maybe Symes is smarter than he looks."

"You mean he'll think we're watching him?"

Laredo nodded. "It's possible."

Near dark a boy showed up with a covered tray. He went into the office and closed the door.

"Food for the prisoners," Laredo said.

The boy did not reappear. He would probably wait and take the tray back, but darkness fell, and still he did not come out.

Pete kicked the wall. "The boy took a message to Moody!"

"He could have gone out a side window," Laredo agreed. "And if so, it proves Moody *is* in town."

Symes had lifted the boy out the window with a sealed note for Marty Nevers. Two men had come looking for Matt, and he had said Moody was not in town. Symes thought they were government agents.

Marty smoked a cigarette and stared at the note. They could expect government agents to come looking for the reservation money—but why here in Hatcher? Were they snooping in every town, hoping to turn up something? The reward was substantial—maybe that was it.

He thought he could trust Symes to keep his mouth shut. The man was a rabbit and knew a bullet awaited him if he said a wrong word.

He put a match to the note and said nothing to the others.

Lem loved to gamble at cards and usually came away a winner. But neither Marty nor T.R. spent much time in the downstairs saloon. Marty took advantage of the inactivity to sleep. T.R. was usually busy with Hester or one of the other girls. He even played cards with them in their rooms, a game called strip poker, which he told the girls was all the rage in New Orleans.

When Matt was awake Marty sat with him for hours, talking, planning, and discussing other big jobs. It was Matt's desire, he said, to accumulate a large amount of money and retire from the outlaw game for good and all. He would buy a ranch somewhere and raise stock, maybe horses.

Privately, Marty thought it was a wild dream. Matt Moody was not the kind to retire. He was very vain; he wanted people to know who he was! The fact that people now thought he was dead galled him. He was eager to show them otherwise. He wanted to come back from the "dead" with a big job—even bigger than the Indian reservation robbery—if they could find such a one.

Toby Rogers was enjoying himself in Hatcher. It was the first time in several years that he had been able to sleep when he wanted to and played when he wanted to. And he had plenty of money from the Jewett robbery.

Before Matt had been shot, they had kept on the move of necessity, and though he enjoyed the active life, this short time he'd spent in the Red Slipper with a warm, willing girl had brought home to him what he'd been missing. Out on the prairie, riding hell-bent from posses was dangerous, and there was no one to pamper him.

And there was something else. Hester reminded him strongly of Doria in Memphis. He had spent a long time once with Doria and thought of her often. He'd hated to leave her. She had a crazy, wild streak that Hester and the other girls lacked. Hester would do anything he wanted but very casually, as if she were thinking of something else more important. Doria had made him scream and yell—and moan all at the same time. There was no one like her.

If he went to Doria with saddlebags full of greenbacks she would go with him—anywhere. Hadn't she said it once?

Well, he had money now—but not saddlebags bulging with

it. However, he knew where there were great handfuls of cash! The money was hidden behind the old shack on Mrs. Moody's farm. Enough to keep him and Doria for years and years!

What if he went and dug it up?

It would be a hell of a lot easier than the holdup he and Marty were planning. *That* had risks.

He reasoned that since he and Matt and the others had stolen it, the reservation money could be stolen again. Of course, Matt would scream and swear when he found out. He and Lem and Marty would kill him if they caught him— *if* they caught him. But it was a big, wide, untamed country, and there was all the settled east and other countries beyond the ocean. He could change his name, and they'd have no chance to find him, one man among millions.

He could even go down into Texas and do what Matt so often said he wanted to do—buy a ranch and raise stock. And he'd be with Doria.

The more he thought about it, the better it sounded. Hester was beginning to bore him anyway, and she was by far the best of the lot.

Doria was different.

He looked in on Matt. The big man was sitting up, chafing at the bit. He was able to walk about; the doc said he was mending fast. In a couple of weeks he'd be as good as new.

T.R. knew that he'd have to make up his mind in a hurry— do it, or not do it.

That evening with Hester, she was petulant and fussed at him. She asked him for more money, saying he took up all her time. It made him look hard at her, seeing her clearly for what she was, nothing but a saloon whore. How different from Doria!

Early the next morning he went to the stable and rubbed down the roan horse, checking for stone bruises, cuts, saddle galls, and sore mouth. He found none; the horse was in excellent condition. Before the others were up he filled a sack with food: coffee, flour, dried beef, sowbelly, crackers. He would be on the trail a long time. It was a far reach between towns all the way to the Big River. Damn few places to buy more. He wanted to avoid towns anyway, if at all possible. He would be very smart to leave no trace of his passing.

He had said nothing to anyone about Doria or Memphis. When they realized he was gone, how would they know in which direction to look for him? He smiled. He'd say something to Hester about wanting to see someone in Omaha again.

He hid the food sack in the stable. He would go that night.

Chapter Nine

THEIR best bet was to continue to watch the marshal. He was their only lead in the town. Symes hung out at the Red Slipper Saloon, drinking and playing cards, gossiping. But no one they recognized went near him.

Pete said, "If Symes is paid off by Moody, and Moody was staying in that building, Symes would naturally hang out there, wouldn't he? He wouldn't pick another saloon . . . not a little bug like him."

"You figure Moody is in that building?"

"I'd guess so. Somewhere."

Laredo looked it over from the boardinghouse window. The Red Slipper had a restaurant on one side and a dance hall on the other. It was one of the two largest buildings in town. There must be a lot of rooms in it. And Matt Moody could be in any one of them. Pete was probably right.

But how to get in to find out?

They sat in their boardinghouse room and discussed the problem. If they called in the cavalry to surround the place they would look mighty foolish if Moody was *not* there.

Laredo said, "Remember John Fleming told us the important thing was the money, not Moody. His bosses want the money back—then they'll get Moody."

"I don't agree, but where is the money?"

"We figured they stashed it somewhere."

Pete took out the makin's. "Why haven't they got it with them?"

"Of course they might have. Maybe it's under Moody's bed."

Pete rolled the cigarette. "But you don't think it is?"

Laredo smiled. "No, because if they had to make a quick getaway, they could trip over it."

"It's not like a gang like them to keep that much money close by and not split it up. And we know from the past that they don't hang around small towns when they're in the chips." Pete licked the cigarette and felt for a match. "I agree they stashed it somewhere. Maybe on Moody's farm—his mother's farm."

Laredo snapped his fingers. "A very good idea, amigo! Very good indeed! But can you narrow it down a little?"

"Well, it wouldn't be in the house—would it?"

"Ummm. The farm must be fifty or sixty acres." Laredo mused, tapping his chin. "I don't care for the odds. It might take us a hundred years to find it."

"We could set a gang of men to digging. . . ."

"Then Moody would show up and shoot them."

"Only if the money *was* there."

Laredo sighed deeply. "We're getting nowhere. The money could be somewhere else, and Moody and the others are the only ones who know where it is. John Fleming's superiors have no idea at all what they're asking. We have to find out through Moody. We get Moody, *then* we get the money. Not the other way round."

"And it won't be easy," Pete said. "We don't even know where Moody is."

"You said he was in the Red Slipper building."

Pete grinned. "So I did. Let's go back and watch it."

They spent hours in the saloon, and when they saw Dr. Weaver enter with his bag and go up the back steps, they were even more convinced Moody was there.

"Weaver lied to us," Pete said. "He's been treating Moody all along."

59

Dr. Weaver was reluctant to talk to them when they faced him later in his office. He ordered them out, but when Pete drew his knife, scowling, Laredo got between them, pushing Pete back, and Weaver caved in, eyeing Pete as if he were a madman.

Yes, he had been treating Matt Moody, but Moody was up and around now. He had been drinking and was in a foul mood when Weaver saw him that day. Moody had been shouting about someone named T.R. and was about to go off in a buckboard. . . .

"Go away from Hatcher?"

Weaver gave a great sigh. "T.R. was one of the gang, and he's disappeared. They haven't seen him for two days."

"Can Moody travel?"

"Oh yes. He's come round rapidly."

"Did they say where they're going?"

Weaver shook his head.

T.R. left Hatcher long before sunup. He could be almost certain no one would notice that he was gone from the town for at least a day. He frequently spent the night with Hester and did not get out of the sack until she did, which was noon or later. His movements did not ordinarily follow a pattern, anyway. He seldom saw Lem from day to day and often did not speak to Marty at all until late at night.

So two days went by before Marty began to ask questions. "Where the hell is T.R.?"

Matt was enraged about T.R. He had no business going off without saying a word. He questioned Hester, and the frightened girl could say only that T.R. had mentioned wanting to see someone in Omaha.

"Why the hell would he go to Omaha?"

Marty didn't know. He thought it unlikely. Omaha was a long journey just to see someone. He was annoyed as hell that T.R. had gone just when they were planning to rob the Chandler messenger. But he said nothing to Matt about that.

None of the other saloon girls knew anything, and neither

did anyone else they talked to. Had someone dry-gulched him and buried the body? T.R. had shot a man named Benson; had his friends shot T.R.? But several bartenders swore that Benson had no close friends, and surely no one would take up another's quarrel to face a gunman like T.R.

It was a mystery, and Matt hated mysteries. He was a direct man. He liked direct answers, and there was no answer to T.R.'s disappearance.

Unless . . .

He woke in the middle of the night thinking about it. Could T.R. be double-crossing all of them? Could he be on the way to the farm to dig up the money?

He routed out a half-drunk Marty to yell at him. Marty agreed through a haze that yes, it was possible. They woke Lem up and started out at first light.

Laredo wired John Fleming at once, asking for any information at all concerning Toby Rogers, called T.R. The man had disappeared from Hatcher. Where was he likely to go?

Fleming wired back that the information he had was unreliable. Rogers had given several different towns as his birthplace. One was San Antonio, and another was Memphis. However, he had spent time in jail in Marion, a town near Memphis, so Fleming thought that the more likely.

Pete asked, "Why would he go back to Memphis just because he was born there?"

"Maybe he had a letter from a relative and wanted to return for some reason."

"How would the relative know where to write him?"

Laredo grinned. "Because T.R. wrote him first."

"Well, it's on the way—if we're going to the Moody farm."

Laredo took his hat off and ran his fingers through his tawny hair. "The farm is a hunch bet. But can you think of a better one?"

"Not today. Let's go."

* * *

T.R. approached the farm at a walk and halted under the trees to study the little house. He could see no one stirring. There was a buckboard standing near the barn and two mules in the near corral. Mrs. Moody was probably in the house in her rocking chair by the fire. A thin column of gray smoke rose from the chimney in the still air. If the hired man was around, he must be in the barn.

He turned the horse after a bit and went down across the south field to the little flat-roofed shack. It was in a scattering of trees and was gradually rotting away. The door was off, and it smelled of wild animals inside. T.R. got down and walked around the shack. Matt had said he'd buried the money behind it, but he could see no evidence of a recent filled-in hole. Of course, it had been a while, and the ground was now weedy.

He went into the shack and looked for a shovel. Nothing. He swore. How in hell was he going to dig up the money without a shovel? There were some sticks on the ground, but it would take a month to dig a hole with them. Even his knife was of little use. The area behind the shack was some ten feet square, and the sack might be anywhere in that space. Matt hadn't been very definite, saying he'd buried it in the dark.

He looked across the field. There was certainly a shovel in the barn.

He mounted the roan and rode back to the house, halting again in the trees. There was a buggy in front of the house, with a horse cropping grass. Mrs. Moody had visitors.

T.R. swore again at his luck and got down to wait.

But the visitors stayed and stayed. Finally T.R. circled the house at a distance and came up on the barn from the rear. But when he crept close he could hear someone singing to himself inside.

Son of a bitch. He decided to wait until dark.

He rode back to the trees by the front, and in an hour two women and a boy came out and climbed in the buggy. They drove off toward the town.

Much later a man emerged from the barn, hooked up one

of the mules, talked to Mrs. Moody for a time, then drove off toward town. T.R. circled around again to the barn.

It was dark when he entered. He struck a match and found a shovel leaning against the wall. Grabbing it, he climbed on the roan and rode back to the old shack, swearing at all the wasted time.

He dared not show a light, so, beginning in the center of the area, he started digging in the dark. Two hours later he still had found nothing. Unused to such work, he sat down on the edge of the hole he'd made and rested.

What if Matt hadn't buried the money here as he'd told them? Would he do such a thing? No, probably not, because he planned to lead them here and dig it up when they were all together.

He worked for another hour; then, tired out, he ate something and rolled up in his blankets and slept.

He made a fire in the morning, under the trees, so his smoke would not be noticed, boiled coffee and broiled meat. Then he went back to work digging. The ground was not hard, but not soft either; the sun had been baking it since the last rain a while ago.

By nightfall he had dug up perhaps half the area behind the old shack—with nothing to show for it but holes. Matt had said: Behind the shack, but not how far or how close. Maybe he should have gone through with the plan of robbing the messenger with Marty. But this had seemed such a sure thing—and was turning out not to be.

He worried, too, how long it would be till they found he had gone—how long till they suspected he had come here? If they did suspect his whereabouts, they could arrive at any time. And when they came, it would be quietly.

That night T.R. left the shack and rolled up in his blankets half a mile away in a copse of trees.

In the morning he debated digging again. He had an itchy feeling between his shoulder blades. They wouldn't hesitate if they found him here, and they'd bury him in one of the holes he'd dug.

But the lure of the money was too great. He returned to

behind the shack and dug furiously—and in a few hours struck something with his shovel! It proved to be the sack! He pulled it out of the ground but had no time to open it.

Riders and a wagon were coming along the road near the Moody house. He could hear them clearly in the still morning air. It had to be Matt and the others! What to do?

The sack was heavy, and his horse was a hundred yards away in the trees. He would have to walk or run upright, carrying the sack, and they might see him.

Grunting, he tossed the sack to the flat roof of the shack. It could not be seen from the ground. Then he scuttled along in the brush to the roan horse and led it quietly away.

But when he mounted and headed eastward a rifle shot followed him, then several more. He had been seen!

The chase lasted for several hours, but he drew away from them finally; the roan was stronger and faster. He had left them far behind by nightfall.

He veered south, thinking he would circle back and pick up the money sack—after letting some time go by. In two days he saw the lights of a town as dusk fell. It was a little burg called Loudon—a main street, two saloons, a grub shop, and not much else, not even a hotel. He put his horse in the stable and went across the street to the saloon, the White Dog.

A brawl was going on in the middle of the saloon floor, tables pushed back. In a circle of spectators two men, stripped to the waist, were punching each other with bare fists, fighting to pass the hat.

T.R. had seen this often. He had a beer at the bar and watched them go to it. One man was larger, and he finally knocked his opponent down and was declared the winner.

He was a big brute, black-haired with a heavy black mustache and bulging muscles; possibly, T.R. thought, the town bully, from the way he strutted. He came to the bar loudly calling for beer, pushing T.R. aside.

Instantly T.R. threw the contents of his beer mug on him. The bully looked around in surprise, doubled up his fists, roared in rage, and swung viciously at T.R. As the bully charged him T.R. stepped back, pulled his pistol, and fired twice, directly into the other's chest. The big man fell against him, and T.R. pushed the body off onto the floor.

The saloon was suddenly quiet. Men stared at him, a few coughing and shuffling chairs as T.R. pushed out the brass and reloaded.

Someone knelt and felt for a pulse, then shook his head.

A man with a star badge on his coat stepped out of the crowd and asked T.R. for his pistol.

"I got t'take you over to the jail, friend. Matter of form. I seen it all, and the magistrate'll set you free in the mornin'. You comin' peaceable?"

T.R. grunted and handed over the Colt. "I wasn't going to let him pound me."

"I don't blame you. Neither would I." The deputy motioned to the bartenders. "Git him out onto the walk, and send somebody for Stringer."

The jail was a two-cell affair built of fieldstones and wood. T.R. was the only occupant. He was locked into a cold cell that had an iron cot and a rickety chair. He sat on the cot and sighed, pulling his coat closer about him. The man he'd shot *had* been the town bully, and no one was particularly sorry to see the last of him, according to the deputy. He was assured there would be no trouble about his release in the morning.

But the magistrate could not see him the next day. He had a full slate, the deputy apologized. But the next day . . .

. . . Marty Nevers walked into the jail.

Chapter Ten

T.R. was lying on the cot when Marty stepped up to the bars. "Hello, kid."

Toby sat up, glancing at the door to see if Matt was there.

Marty said, "Matt's too mad to come in here right now. Where's the money?"

"I haven't got any money."

"Come on, T.R. We seen where you dug. Matt says you found it."

"Well, he's wrong. I didn't. It's still there."

Marty frowned at the younger man. The marshal had said T.R. had nothing on him. His horse was in the stable and nothing on it either, only the saddle and rifle. The stable owner said T.R. didn't leave nothing behind. He said, "You ditched it somewhere."

"No, I didn't find it, dammit! If I found it I'd have it with me!"

Marty considered. Maybe Matt had been wrong. It was a big area behind the shack, and only part of it had been dug up. Matt could be wrong—he was so damned mad when he saw the digging he couldn't think straight. The money sack *could* still be in the undug part.

He said, "That was a goddamn dumb thing to do, Toby. And all us trustin' you like that."

T.R. shrugged. "It was a gamble that didn't pay off, that's all."

"Oh, there'll be a payoff," Marty promised. He went to the door and out. The marshall gave him his gun back, and he went down the street to the stable.

Matt growled, "Well, whad he say?"

"Said he never got to it. It's still there in the ground."

Matt scowled and kicked the side of the building, but Marty could tell he was unsure. Maybe it was still there. Maybe . . .

Laredo and Pete Torres followed the riders and the buckboard from far back. The wagon left plain tracks that could not be hidden. And they traveled slowly because the road was terrible, and the wagon would shake itself to pieces if they hurried. The weather was getting better and better; summer was approaching.

The three men went directly to the Moody farm, arriving in the morning. They did not go to the house but turned south across the fields toward an old shack. Laredo and Pete could not get close enough to see what was happening, but there were half a dozen rifle shots, then nothing.

Laredo said, "They scared someone off—probably T.R."

"And now they're chasing after him."

They paused at the shack and saw where someone had dug up a goodly portion of ground behind it.

"That's where the reservation money was," Laredo said. "You were right. It was here on the farm."

"But T.R.'s got it now, and he's on his way to the Mexican border."

"If Moody and the others don't catch him."

They followed the chase, staying well back as before. If T.R. had the money, and it looked likely, they might be able to get in on the finish.

If the money had been buried behind the shack, it meant that probably it was intact, that none had been spent. John Fleming's bosses would appreciate that.

The chase led them eventually, several days later, to the little town of Loudon, where they heard about the shooting of the town bully. A stranger had ridden into town and gotten himself into a fracas and pulled a pistol. The bully was dead, and the stranger had been put in the jailhouse to await the decision of the magistrate.

When they visited the marshal in his jail office he told them, "That's a funny thing." He took off his hat to scratch his head. "The feller said a bunch was waiting to increase his weight with lead. One of them come in here in fact, talked with the feller. He asked me t'have his horse brought around to the back of the jail. Well, the magistrate said they was no reason t'hold him, so I did it. What the hell, I d'want no more shootin' than I have to put up with. And he took off like a bear shot in the butt."

"Did he give you a name?"

"Said 'is handle was Tom Summers. But they was a T.R. burned into his saddle."

"Did he have a sack with him?"

"Ever'body asks that question. No, he didn't have nothing with him. What you want him for?"

Laredo smiled. "We want the sack."

T.R. had gotten clean away, and Moody suspected the marshal had been a help to him in that. But with his picture on file and possibly a poster in the office, he could hardly protest. There was no telling which way T.R. had gone, so Matt and the others returned to the farm.

Matt had been positive, when he looked at the ground behind the shack, that T.R. had found the sack of money. But if he didn't have it in Loudon, maybe he hadn't found it after all. It could still be in the ground because they *had* scared him off.

He had Marty and Lem dig up the rest of the area.

When every possible inch was uncovered, the money sack had not been found. Could someone else have dug it up? But who else would know?

"That sombitch T.R. got it," Matt swore. "Somehow he hornswoggled us."

Marty asked, "Did he ever talk about going anywhere in particular? And I don't mean Omaha!"

They shook their heads. No one could remember anything of the sort.

There was no point remaining at the farm. Matt decided to return to Hatcher and the comfort of Velma's establishment. He was very down in the mouth. The reservation money had been part of his retirement fund. . . . And now it was gone.

He was very hard to talk to for days. He drank too much and shouted at anyone who came near. Once he staggered down the upstairs hall firing his pistol at the walls.

But when he was sober, he and Marty talked of various possibilities. Matt was sure they could find and rob a government payroll, since the government paid off in cash. But which payroll?

Then one day Marty broached the idea he and T.R. had planned. The local messenger was still riding to Chandler every week carrying large sums of cash.

Matt was instantly interested. "Where the hell you learn all this?"

"I been nosing around. Didn't want to bring it up till I had more facts."

"You got enough now?"

Marty lit a cigarette. "No. The messenger goes different days. There don't seem to be a pattern for it. I think he leaves at night from the livery, so we got to watch it."

Marty spread out a map. "Chandler's here, about eighty miles by the road. Going across country might cut off fifteen. Most of it's high plains, but there's these hilly parts. . . ." He pointed them out.

Matt asked, "How long they been doing this?"

"I don't know. But prob'ly a year or two."

"Then the messenger's laid down some trails, sure. If he makes that trip fifty times a year, he got to. And you figger he changes horses?"

"I think he has to if he going to make any schedule. We ought to find that way station."

Matt nodded. "That's the first thing. We'll slide out easy in the morning and have a look."

"How you feel about riding?"

Matt made a face. "Doc says I'm good as new."

Howie and Bob Flagg got drunk in the Osage Saloon in Yorkville on the last of Flagg's money. When he reached in his jeans, the pocket was empty; he was broke. He turned it out to show Howie.

"But hell, I c'n git more," Flagg said. "I c'n collect the goddamn reward on Matt Moody. I shot 'im, din't I?"

"Sure you shot 'im," Howie agreed. "I seen you do it."

Flagg laughed and pounded the other on the back. "You seen me do it? Where the hell was you?"

Howie was a little fuzzy. "Din't I seen you?"

"Maybe you did at that. Where the hell we gonna collect the reward?"

A bartender leaned over the bar toward Flagg. "You shot Matt Moody?"

"Yeh, I did," Flagg said, trying to keep the other in focus. "Now'm goin' to collect the reward."

"You got to have a body."

"What?"

The bartender explained. "If you wanna collect the reward, you got to have the body."

Flagg looked puzzled. "Body's back there on the floor."

"Well, you got to have the body, or they ain't going to pay you a cent."

"Izzat true?"

"Absolutely. They got to have evidence."

Flagg turned and shoved Howie. "We got to go get the body."

"Awright. Where izzit?"

"It's lyin' on the floor. Come on." Flagg headed for the door, dragging Howie along.

As the two went out the door to the street the bartender shook his head and said to no one in particular, "They get

70

some drinks in 'em, and they dunno what the hell they doing. Imagine him sayin' he shot Matt Moody!''

Marty was sure the messenger did not leave Hatcher on the same day every week—he would make it random if he were the boss. So it would be necessary to keep a watch on the livery and be ready to intercept the man.

Then one afternoon Lem happened to be in the stable and saw the younger Johnson, the owner's son, brushing down a fine bay horse, paying particular attention to the hoofs.

Lem went back to the saloon and said to Marty and Matt, "I bet you he's riding to Chandler tonight."

Matt growled. "We ain't found the way station yet. We got to do that before he goes next week."

Chapter Eleven

T.R. had disappeared without a trace. If he had the money sack, they had lost him.

But Matt Moody, Lem, and Marty Nevers were easy to follow back to the farm. It never seemed to occur to them to look over their shoulders.

From a distance Laredo and Pete watched the trio digging behind an old shack. But as far as they could determine with binoculars, the diggers found nothing. If they had dug up the sack, they would certainly have celebrated.

Pete said, "My money is on T.R. He must have found the reservation money and stashed it somewhere."

"So we assume this bunch doesn't have it and doesn't know where it is."

"I think so."

Laredo pursed his lips. "Is it possible a third party got in somehow and ran off with it?"

"No, it's not possible."

"You're very sure."

"How would a third party know? But, T.R. didn't have the money at Loudon."

Laredo scratched his chin. "Someone's got to know where it is. Maybe a holdup man took it from T.R."

Pete looked at him. "Does that sound likely to you?"

"No . . . but where is it? We thought Moody would lead

us to it, but apparently Moody doesn't know any more than we do. And T.R.'s gone up the flue.''

Pete fiddled with a tobacco sack. "We've got to find T.R. He's the answer.''

T.R. rode south from Loudon, putting as much distance between himself and the town as he could. No telling what Matt and the others would do. Matt had no patience at all and an enormous amount of faith in his six-gun.

Marty had looked as if he half believed the story that the money sack was still in the ground at the Moody farm. But it wouldn't take them long to dig up the rest of the ground, if they decided to, and learn the truth.

His only chance, as he saw it, was to disappear—for the time being. Let them think he had gone for good. And hope and pray no one climbed up onto the roof of the shack.

But T.R. had to return to the farm sooner or later. That would be the easy part. Then he'd just slide the sack off the roof and be on his way. He'd point east to Memphis—and Doria—and leave the old life behind.

Of course, he dared not stay away from the shack too long. As he rode he told himself over and over that probably no one had climbed to the roof, since the shack had been built years ago. Why should they do it now? Unless old Mrs. Moody decided to use it for something. The thought made him groan.

He paused at the first town he came to and spent several days. But then he was in the saddle again, unable to stay away. One hundred and fifty thousand dollars waited for him. It was all his—all he had to do was pick it up. He remembered the feel of the rough canvas in his hands, rough and heavy. Full of greenbacks!

He approached the farm from the south and was annoyed to see men working there. Someone was plowing with a two-mule team, and a gang of men was clearing the fields between the house and shack, burning stacks of weeds. The smoke drifted lazily off to the east.

It hadn't occurred to him that when Matt spoke of the place

as a farm that it was a *farm* that raised crops. He swore, watching the men work. Was Matt there, in the house? Maybe he had started all this activity. One never knew what Matt might do.

He stayed out of sight. Late at night he should be able to climb onto the shack roof.

But the workers camped there, near the shack. They put up a row of brown tents, built fires, and looked as if they were going to stay a while. If he tried to climb onto the shack roof, would they hear him? Probably. There was no ladder anywhere near. He might stand on the saddle and scramble up. . . .

But if they heard him and raised a ruckus and Matt were at the house, he would quickly guess who had returned, and then he'd know the money was stashed somewhere near—he might look on the roof!

T.R. knew he could not take the chance.

But his nerves were getting tighter and rawer.

The stories of the outlaw Matt Moody's death were many and varied. Some insisted the man was not dead at all but merely recovering from a wound. Others scoffed at that, saying a funeral had taken place. It had been reported in the local weekly.

A few enterprising reporters had dug up a story about a man named Bob Flagg. Flagg had been bragging in saloons that he'd shot Moody. Interested listeners bought him drinks to hear about it. Others said that Flagg was known to be loose with facts, and his stories *did* differ. He forgot what he'd said before.

But a man named Larson heard the tales and decided Matt Moody was a fascinating character, someone whose story was worth telling. Once that story had been written, he had it published as a series of nationally-run newspaper stories that paid no attention to facts. The first story, "Matt Moody, Killer of the Plains" was avidly read in the effete east, and some of the copies drifted west, one as far as Hatcher where the paper was delivered to Velma at the Red Slipper.

Moody could barely read and write, so Velma read the story to him. He was fascinated with the deeds he had not done. To him the story was high praise. Velma thought it trash and explained that someone had merely used his name and notoriety to sell copies. However, Matt was convinced he was a celebrity . . . and a hero.

He had the local photographer take his picture with two six-guns strapped about his middle, a rifle in his arms, and the book held prominently. He had the picture framed and hung in his room.

The photographer sent copies of the picture east where they were printed in the dailies, laying to rest the tales of Moody's death.

Marty Nevers deplored Matt's ill-advised act, and the reward for Moody was increased to four thousand dollars, dead or alive.

Marty and Lem, in hours of riding, discovered the location of the way station. It was a shacky house and corral five or six miles from the road in the hills. Only one man was in attendance.

When the watch on the stable told them the messenger was about to leave, the three rode to the way station. Matt called out, and when the man came to the door, Matt shot him down.

"Drag 'im inside, and put the horses round the back where they won't be seen."

Then they took up positions in the house and waited. They would shoot the rider when he appeared and leave both bodies in the house.

The messenger did not arrive till after midnight. He stopped in the dark and gave a peculiar whistle.

"Jesus!" Marty said. "They got a sign! Now what the hell we do?"

"Knock 'im off the horse!" Matt said, growling.

But the messenger was invisible in the dark. They pumped shots where they thought the whistle had come from, then ran for the horses. But there was no chance of catching the elusive messenger. He knew every fold of ground and easily evaded them.

After an hour of fruitless rushing about, there was nothing to do but return to Hatcher empty-handed. Matt was in a foul mood. He blamed his men for not knowing the countersign. They should have thought of it, he snarled, though he had not thought of it either. A man had died for nothing, and the chances of robbing the messenger again were very slim. Certainly they would change the system.

But at least no one knew who had made the attempt. If Velma suspected, she said nothing.

Now that Matt was well again, he was restless. He was a vain man; the notoriety given him by the novel had seeped into his blood like a disease, and he hankered for more. And the way to get more was to become the Killer of the Plains and the most wanted outlaw the book depicted.

"We got to get back to banks," Matt said. "That's where we made our money. Robbin' messengers is too goddamn complicated."

"But he's prob'ly got more money on him than five banks."

"*If* we could catch 'im. One man in the dark on a fast horse . . ." Matt shook his head. "And he prob'ly knows ever' prairie dog by his first name."

Lem asked, "We giving up on T.R.?"

Matt swung round. "No—but where the hell you going to start looking for him?"

"He dug the money up," Lem persisted.

"And ran off with it," Matt said, viciously.

"He didn't have it in Loudon," Marty remarked. "He stashed it somewhere."

Lem agreed. "Somewhere between the farm and Loudon."

Matt curled his lip. "That's one hell of a lot of territory. You going to search it all?"

"It's a lot of money, too," Lem said softly.

Matt stared at him. "What you suggesting? You really want to go lookin' for it?"

"Wait a minute," Marty said. "If he stashed it, he didn't have much time to figger a good, safe place. Maybe Lem is right, we *could* find it. It's worth a try—that much money. Let's go back to the farm and start from there."

Matt paced the room. "All right," he said finally. "We'll give it a try."

"If we find it," Marty said, grinning, "it beats robbin' banks."

Laredo and Pete returned to Loudon, the last place T.R. had been seen. Where would he go from there?

"If he's got the money," Pete said, "he'll make tracks for some place a long way from here."

"All right, let's assume that's correct. How does he carry the money?"

"What?"

"He can't take it into a town in a heavy sack stamped with big black letters: 'U.S. Government Property.' "

"He'll put it in a gunny sack."

Laredo nodded. "So we ask about a gent with a fat gunny sack."

"He'll put it in a carpetbag as soon as he can find one."

"I think so, too. Next thing—where does he go from here? Does he take the stage or go to the railroad?"

Pete said, "The railroad is faster, but it's a long way from Loudon. I say he takes the stage."

"Loudon is not on a stage line."

They inquired. The nearest stage was at Hepple, thirty miles south. It took a day to get there, but when they showed the stage operator the picture of Toby Rogers, the man shook his head. "Haven't seen him."

"He'll be carrying a gunny sack or a carpetbag."

"Most folks do," the operator said. "I haven't seen this one."

Pete asked, "Do you see everyone who gets on the stage?"

"I sell the tickets." The man nodded. "I see everyone, yes."

"Has anyone else asked you about this man?"

"No. No one."

They thanked him and went to the nearest saloon. Pete said, "The nearest railroad is about a hundred miles from here. Would he ride all that way rather than take the stage-coach?"

"I doubt it. Didn't you say he was in a hurry?"

"I'd think he would be."

Laredo took off his hat. "But he didn't take the stage." He watched Pete roll a brown cigarette. "What if he doesn't have the reservation money?"

"I thought we agreed he did."

"Well, look at what he did—he should have taken the stage. Why didn't he?"

Pete lit the cigarette and puffed thoughtfully. "If he doesn't have the money . . . you're saying he stashed it before he got to Loudon."

"So he went back for it."

"Ahhh."

"Doesn't that figure?"

"It's a very interesting idea that ought to be explored."

Chapter Twelve

T.R. watched the farm workers at a distance. Several men were working near the shack, though he could not tell what they were doing. He could see only far-off figures moving about.

He pulled his revolver, flicked open the loading gate, and rolled the cylinder down his arm, looking at the brass. He could ride to the shack and probably take the money sack by force, no matter how many of them were facing him. Would farm workers be armed? Of course not.

But if he did that, could he get away? The local law would raise a posse consisting of most of the men in the area—the reward would attract dozens. He might not be able to stay ahead of them, and the publicity would be horrendous. His picture would be posted everywhere! Even in Memphis.

No, the smart thing had to be to get at the money sack somehow without anyone knowing. He put the pistol away.

He found a good place to make camp in a cave in the rocks several miles away. Each day he crept as close as he dared, to watch the workers. Several times at night he moved in close to the shack, close enough to hear them talking by the fires. The row of tents they had put up, and the outdoor ovens and fireplaces they had built, seemed to say that they intended to stay all summer.

One night he was challenged. Someone had seen him and yelled, firing a rifle. T.R. ducked away and listened to the ruckus. Men were up and out of the tents, rushing here and there with lanterns, probably looking for robbers.

He stayed clear for the next few days. His food supplies were low anyhow, so he saddled up and rode west to the next town, not daring to go into Peryton. The place was hardly a town, only a few weather-beaten buildings at a crossroads. It had a general store, a deadfall, a blacksmith, and not much else. There were a few scattered houses and no particular street.

He told the store owner what news he could remember from Loudon, filled two sacks with foodstuffs, and mentioned that he was heading south to his home in Austin. Three old-timers sitting on the porch studied him as he rode away.

In Peryton, Laredo wired John Fleming to bring him up to date. T.R. had double-crossed the Moody gang and had disappeared. Moody and the others did not seem to know where the reservation money was, and he and Pete had doubts about T.R. having it either. It was probably hidden somewhere.

Their efforts to locate T.R. had come to a dead end, but *if* T.R. had hidden the money he would certainly return for it, and they hoped to run into him then. This was all speculation, Laredo stressed.

Fleming wired that if they were positive Moody did not have the money, why not arrest Moody, Lem, and Nevers?

Laredo replied that they could not be absolutely positive, and anyhow it might take a well-armed group to bring in the Moody gang. Also, if the Moody gang was killed, and they *did* have the money, it might be lost forever.

Fleming wired that the matter was getting very complicated. He would put out posters with T.R.'s photograph. Perhaps that would help.

Laredo thought it would. He and Pete were returning to Hatcher and would report again soon.

* * *

He and Pete discussed bringing in the Moody gang. Not a particularly easy task. They were three gunmen, dangerous as teased rattlers, and they were watchful and suspicious.

The local law, Bill Symes, town marshal, was doubtless in Moody's pay and could not be trusted. The nearest United States Marshal was based in Ettinger, five or six days' ride west. By the time they got there, convinced the marshal to send a posse, and returned, Moody might not be anywhere near Hatcher.

All three probably would have to be arrested together. If one were caught, it would alert the others. And where would they hold one of them? Not in the local jail.

Pete thought it would not help in the search for the missing money to arrest Moody. "He might even lead us to T.R."

That was possible.

They went to the Red Slipper again to look it over, but dared not ask about Moody. Strangers asking for Matt Moody would not be well received and would point themselves out.

A boy was cleaning floors, it being a slow time, as they sipped beer at the bar. When the boy picked up his mop and bucket and went out, they followed him without seeming to and stopped him some distance from the saloon.

Laredo gave the astonished lad a dollar. He had not seen Moody for days, the boy told them, and he had heard talk that Moody and his friends were out of town. He promised to tell them what he could in the future.

They were both surprised when the boy sought them out that evening to say that, while he had been helping the waiters in the restaurant, he had overheard a conversation at a table that Moody and the others had gone north and were not expected back in Hatcher.

Laredo gave him another dollar and asked him to say nothing to anyone.

"Why is he going north?" Pete asked when the boy had left.

"Maybe he's up to his old tricks."

"You mean banks?"

"Certainly I mean banks. Moody and his friends have to

live as well as anyone else. That's the kind of work they do, rob banks."

Matt, and especially Marty, gave it out to the bartenders and casual friends that the three of them were on their way north, hinting that they had something special in mind.

When they rode out at dawn they took the road north for several miles before abruptly turning east, heading for the Moody farm.

When they halted for the night, Marty said, "After T.R. dug up the money, he probably hid it in the first mile, because we scared him off. All we have to do is look for a good spot. It has to be someplace he can find again easy."

"It was in the dark," Lem put in.

"That's right. So it ought to be even easier for us."

Matt asked, "Why d'you figger it has to be in the first mile or so?"

"Because he knew we were right on his tail. He didn't want to be caught with the money sack, did he? He'd get rid of it as soon as he could. It's in a tree or a hole in the ground, or in some brush. . . ."

"Maybe somebody else found it," Matt said darkly.

"Not likely," Marty replied. "Damn few people ride through the brush where there's no roads."

When they reached the farm, Lem and Marty bunked in the barn room. Sam, the hired man, had brought in workers to clear the fields and plow according to Matt's instructions. Sam spoke with Matt about buying cattle. The price of cows up north on the railroad was much higher than it had been several years ago. A herd of ten or twelve thousand, when driven to market, would pay very well.

It was honest work, but Matt was not averse to it. He was broad-minded when it came to money.

The farm could easily be increased to three or four times its present size, Sam said. The land was cheap, and he knew where cows could be had for a fair price. Matt told him to go ahead.

The second day they were there the three wasted no time

and started out as soon as it was light, moving from the old shack, eastward, following T.R.'s tracks as they remembered them. They were very thorough and found half a dozen likely spots, but no money sack.

However, Marty was encouraged. "I think we're getting close."

Except that in three days of searching they found nothing. They rode almost to Loudon then went back over the same ground again, taking more time, but still came up empty.

Even Marty was then discouraged. "He must of had it with him when he went into the town."

"Or maybe he left it at the edge of town." Lem said.

"And picked it up again when he rode out."

There was nothing to do but return to the farm, tired and bedraggled. T.R. was gone and the money with him.

"He is probably in Kansas City or some big eastern town," Marty said, "living like a king on our money, telling folks he made it in cattle."

But T.R. was not five miles away in his cave in the rocks. Each night he slipped through the dark to the farm to see the progress of the clearing and plowing.

On one dark and misty night he crossed the field on foot and approached the shack cautiously. No guard had been posted, and he did not encounter a dog. He could even hear snores from one of the worker's tents. It was a still, peaceful night.

He discovered that men had been working on the shack itself, making it into a small bunkhouse. They had put in a floor and framed up the door and window and were building bunks along three inside walls.

He found and carried a workbench close to one of the walls and was about to climb up when he heard the snarl and turned to see the approaching dog. Grabbing up a stout club he kept the dog at bay, backing into the field. The dog only snarled and growled, dodging the quick blows, and T.R. was able to reach his horse.

He wanted to kill the damned dog and go back, but he

dared not shoot it. And if he got off the horse with his knife, it might be a terrible mistake. The dog might be much quicker than he, and he might come off second-best and have need of a doc. Also, this one might not be the only watchdog. He rode away swearing.

He crept as close as he dared the next day and watched the carpenters sawing and hammering by the shack. No one climbed to the roof; apparently, it did not leak. But he saw three dogs wandering about. When one stopped and looked in his direction, T.R. crept back.

He was astonished to see Matt, Lem, and Marty ride past the shack and disappear to the east. Were they looking for him? Probably.

Laredo and Pete Torres rode north from Hatcher to the next small town, Ryeville. It took a very short time to learn that Moody and his friends had not been seen there. The outlaws had probably circled the town and gone on. There was almost nothing to rob in a burg like Ryeville, not for a gang like Moody's.

They had a choice after Ryeville, according to the crude map they consulted. There were two towns: Beale, slightly to the west, and Onenburg, off to the east. Beale might be the closest, they were told. It was definitely the larger and was on the telegraph.

They decided to ride to Beale.

It proved to be the county seat and was even larger than Hatcher. The county sheriff had a large office near the courthouse. He was a big, paunchy man with a handlebar mustache and fishy eyes. He was dressed in a baggy store suit with a silver watch chain across his ample middle and was in a hurry to get to court. They could talk to his chief deputy, he told them as he rushed out.

The deputy was named Elkhorn, a stringy, bald man who shared the sheriff's notion that Matt Moody could not possibly be in his town without him knowing.

"Moody ain't the kind t'hide hisself under a bushel basket."

Laredo asked, "What if he's planning a job in your town? Wouldn't he come in nice and quiet?"

Elkhorn squinted at them. "You fellers know something we ought to know?"

"We've been told Moody is coming in this direction," Laredo replied. "Is there anything in town that would interest the Moody gang?"

The deputy regarded them with brooding eyes. "Two banks, but they're both well guarded. Moody'd play hell gettin' anything outa them. Where'd you hear about him?"

"Back in Hatcher. There's nothing else?"

"I don't see him robbin' no grocery stores—do you?"

"Does the stage carry money boxes?"

Elkhorn shrugged his thin shoulders. "Yes, but they don't tell us about it mostly. They got their own shotgun guards."

"No big payrolls in town?"

"Nothing that would attract him. You got the wrong town. Besides, we can raise a posse in ten minutes. We'd put Matt Moody in Boot Hill like that!" He snapped his fingers.

"Thanks," Laredo said. "Guess you would."

When they went out to the street Pete remarked that the deputy seemed a big-mouth. People had bragged before about putting Moody in a six-foot hole. He was still kicking.

"But he might be right about there being nothing here for Moody."

"Let's have a look at the banks."

There were two, as the deputy had said, and they were both definitely well guarded. One, in fact, was directly across the street from the sheriff's office. The other had a curious arrangement of doors, with shotgun guards high up where they could see but not easily be seen. Someone had gone to enormous trouble to make the place robber-proof.

They sat in their hotel room that night convinced that Moody was not in town. The lawmen were probably right.

"We were snookered back in Hatcher," Laredo said. "Moody told everyone he was going north. We should have been more suspicious."

"We thought we had good information. He was clever about it."

Laredo sighed. "Outlaws are like Indians. If you think a redskin is doing one thing, he is sure as hell doing something else. So where did Moody go?"

Pete grinned. "Anywhere but north."

Chapter Thirteen

"**B**ANKS," Matt said. "Banks are the thing. Who else got money like the banks? Let's stop fooling around trying to find that money sack. I got to buy some land and cows."

"All right," Marty agreed. "You got a bank in mind?"

"Hell, no. We got to look around."

They pored over maps, talking about the various prospects. When they came out of the barn, Sam was just turning in from the road with Dr. Shipley sitting beside him on the buckboard seat.

"What's this?" Matt asked, looking at Shipley.

The physician stared at him in surprise. "Your mother's been ailing for months. You don't know it?"

"She never complains about nothing."

Shipley shook his head and went into the house.

Sam said, "I been bringin' him out here ever' week, Mr. Matt."

"What's wrong with her?"

"Doc says it's the wastin' disease. Ain't you noticed how she gettin' thinner and thinner?"

Matt swore. No, he hadn't noticed. He took her for granted. Growling under his breath, he went into the house. Dr. Shipley was sitting beside her bed; there were medicine bottles on the table near them. She did look peaked, now that he paid attention.

After a bit Dr. Shipley came into the kitchen, asking softly, "You have any other kin?"

Matt shook his head. "No—why?"

"I just thought you'd want to notify them."

Matt was puzzled. "What for?"

The doctor sighed. "Because your mother doesn't have much time left."

Matt stared at him. "Much time left . . . ?"

Shipley said, "She's going faster now, and she's getting weaker. I'd say with luck she's got a month, certainly not much longer."

Matt was astonished. "Christ! A month? Ain't there nothing you can do?"

"There's nothing anyone can do now but keep her comfortable. I've given her plenty of laudanum for pain." Shipley moved to the door, closing his bag. "Are you staying here with her—or are you going somewhere?" There was something in his voice that made Matt scowl.

"You say she's got a month to live?"

"Yes—that's a guess of course." Shipley opened the door. "You might make it easier for her if you were here." He went out to the buckboard where Sam was waiting.

Matt decided to stay at the farm. It was perhaps the only time in his life that he'd put his own wishes aside for anyone else, and it felt strange. But Doc Shipley had shocked him with the solemn announcement. His mother was asleep, and he stood in the doorway and stared at her. When she was gone . . . he'd have nobody.

But Lem and Marty were not bound, and they were both restless. They hung around for a time, then they discussed Fairview and decided to ride east to the town and look it over. Maybe they would do a job there.

But first they would go to Camp Hill and recruit one more man.

Camp Hill was a smallish town in the hills, on the side of a wide, gentle slope where someone had found silver a long time ago. Houses, tents, and shacks had been thrown up around the mines, but the miners were long gone. The silver had proved to be little more than a trace, not worth bothering about.

But the town found a purpose and survived; it became an outlaw hangout. No lawman dared go near it for reasons of mortality. Anyone foolish enough to show a badge in the street would be fair game. And the body would be hauled off to the cemetery.

There were five saloons in the little burg and one dance hall, which was part of the Lonestar, owned by Frank Griff. Griff was a grossly fat man who usually lolled in a big leather chair on the main floor, talking, drinking, and doing business. He was the power in Camp Hill.

When Marty and Lem entered the Lonestar and asked for Griff, they were taken to him. Griff hollered, "Hello! Siddown, for crissakes! Where's Matt?"

Marty pulled up a chair. "He stayed back at the farm. His mother's dying."

"Too bad." Griff lit a cigar and glanced toward the door. "Ain't T.R. with you?"

"T.R. went and double-crossed us," Marty told him. "He went south with a sackful of our money."

"T.R. did *that*?" Griff was horrified.

"And when we catch 'im . . ." Marty drew a finger across his throat.

"Son of a bitch! Well, he ain't been here. Haven't heard a word." He slapped Lem's knee. "You all passin' through?"

Lem said, "We come because of T.R. We need us another man."

"That's right," Marty said, nodding. "Somebody that's slick with a gun. You ought to know some."

"Another man?" Griff frowned at the cigar and knocked ashes off the tip. He turned his head and called to a bartender. "Jake—is Luke still in town?"

Jake nodded. "Seen him a while ago this morning."

Griff turned back. "Then Luke's your man. Name's Luke Potter. When you want to see 'im?"

Marty smiled. "Why not now?"

Griff turned back to the bartender. "Send somebody to get Luke." Jake nodded and hurried away.

Luke showed up half an hour later looking as if he'd been asleep. He was lanky and unshaven, dressed like a saddle tramp, but his boots were new, and he peered at each one as Griff introduced them. "Howdy . . . howdy . . ."

He dragged up a chair and sat by Griff. What you folks got in mind?"

"Banks," Marty said. "You innerested in money?"

Luke smiled, showing large, square yellow teeth. "Just the three of us?"

"No, Matt Moody gets a cut."

Luke was surprised. "Moody's comin' along?"

"Maybe. But if he don't, he still gets a cut. You in on them terms?"

Luke frowned, glanced at Griff, then nodded slowly.

Laredo and Pete left Beale and rode to Onenburg, a dusty little town that had no bank at all and not much of anything else. It sunned itself complacently, a collection of weather-beaten storefronts and wooden awnings with faded signs. A black-haired mongrel dog was asleep in the middle of the street when they rode in. The dog lifted one eyelid and went back to sleep.

Pete said, "This isn't Moody's idea of a chance to get rich."

"I'm afraid Moody's given us the slip."

There was no telegraph in the town, nor a stage line, and the papers in the saloon were two weeks old. The town was slowly dying and probably didn't know it, Pete said.

They took the road back to Hatcher. Maybe Moody had never even left.

They talked to the same boy, who told them seriously Moody was not in Hatcher. He hadn't seen Moody or the two men with him, and he'd overheard Velma, the owner of the Slipper, say Moody wouldn't be back—not for a while. But he had no idea where Moody had gone, if he hadn't gone north.

Laredo wired John Fleming and was forced to admit they had lost Moody. He had stolen a march on them. Fleming had no information for them, but it was his opinion that Moody and his gang would not stay out of banks for long. He had been walking into banks with guns for years. Why would he change or stop now?

It was a very good opinion, Laredo said, but not much help.

Fleming's only suggestion was that they concentrate on finding T.R. and the reservation money. He had ordered posters put up everywhere with T.R.'s picture on them. But so far they had not turned up an informer. He was sure the reward would attract someone who needed money.

Concentrate on finding T.R.? Laredo asked Pete, "How do we start looking for him?"

Pete had no ready answer.

Then the stage brought copies of the Peryton weekly into town, and when they scanned a copy they saw the black-edged item: Mrs. Clara Moody, mother of the notorious out-law, Matt Moody, had passed to her Maker on June 16th last. The funeral had been held four days later. The paper did not list the mourners.

Peter said, "I wonder if Matt attended the funeral."

"Why don't we go and ask?"

Marty and Lem discussed the bank at Fairview, but Luke had a better idea, he said. He had looked it over not long ago and thought the bank at Medina was ripe for plucking. It was a damned good prospect. He had been alone at the time, and one man would not have been able to pull if off.

"They got a shotgun guard in a nook above the tellers' cages and another guard on the main floor."

They would have to be eliminated first thing—then it would be easy as spilling beer. The bank served the surrounding ranches and the businesses in town, it being the only one. There was sure to be stacks of money in the safe.

Marty agreed it sounded good, and Lem nodded.

Medina was some fifty miles eastward on the railroad and

partly surrounded by low hills. Luke had gone over the ground, he said, and was positive they would have an easy getaway. The bank was almost in the center of town, but if they were quick they'd be in the hills before a posse could be raised.

They rode to the town, entering it at night and camping several miles away. Marty insisted they spend time deciding on the getaway path. He wanted to know every stick and stone. They would go south, over the hills to the stage road, and follow it, losing their tracks on the well-traveled route.

The town was a prosperous-looking place. It had many stores and saloons, two dance halls, a gambling casino, a large depot by the tracks, and a huge baggage room. There were two side streets and lanes off them with houses, shacks, and sheds, corrals and some tents. There were people everywhere, perhaps as many as a thousand in town. East of town along the tracks was a siding and rows of cattle pens, most of them empty now.

The bank was on a corner, an imposing building with an iron awning over the walk and gold leaf on the windows: MEDINA STATE BANK. They wandered in one at a time to change money and look about casually.

Luke was exactly right about the guards. There were only two.

They sat in a hotel room and discussed what they were to do. The biggest drawback, Marty said, was that they had to shoot the two guards. It was the noise that would possibly alert the town. But there was no way to get the money without shooting. And if some of the townspeople were quick they could cause trouble.

"Especially when we come outa the bank."

"Do banks have back doors?" Lem asked.

Luke didn't know if this one had. They would have to investigate that.

Marty said musingly, "I think we need a diversion."

"*That's* a nine-dollar word."

"Diversion? It means we need a ruckus somewhere else in town so ever'body will think about *it* and not the bank."

Luke wrinkled his forehead. "But they's only three of us. We can't be in two places at once."

Marty tapped his chin. "What about a fire?"

Luke said scornfully, "You can't start a big fire in the middle of town!"

"Not out in the street," Lem said.

"That's right." Marty snapped his fingers. "We c'n do it right here in the hotel." Marty pointed at them. "We bring some tins of kerosene, one at a time, and we pour it all over the hallway and light it. We git out down the back steps."

Lem chuckled. "Hell's fire! That's an idea!"

"Jesus!" Luke said admiringly. "That's smart! They'll be so busy puttin' out the fire they won't think of the bank!"

"That's right." Marty rubbed his hands together. "Tomorrow we each buy kerosene and bring it in from the stable so nobody sees us. We'll start the fire in the afternoon. One of us stays here to light it, then meets us at the bank." He looked at them, and they nodded.

Luke grinned. "That's goin' to be some fire!"

Chapter Fourteen

THE hotel was a two-story frame building, dry as tinder, and would burn fiercely. The hall ran down the center on both floors. The kerosene would make it impossible to put out the fire; it would get a big head start before anyone noticed it, probably.

The tenants, if any were in the rooms, would be able to scramble out the windows, a short drop to the ground. They would add to the confusion when they ran into the street shouting. The more excitement two blocks from the bank, Marty said, the better.

At different times they brought the tins of kerosene into the room, then drew straws to see who would spill the fuel and light it. Lem drew the short straw. Marty and Luke would take the three horses down the alley to the bank corner and wait there for Lem.

The plan went perfectly.

When Marty and Luke left the hotel, Lem opened the door of the room and waited till the hotel seemed quiet. Then he took a deep breath, gritted his teeth, and splashed kerosene over the wall nearest the street. He splashed the walls and the floor as he backed to the rear steps. When he flicked a match to the near puddle he had to run down the steps to escape the searing blast of heat. The fire was a raging inferno in seconds! It crackled and snapped in glee, eating the walls and floor.

Lem ran out to the stable and down the alley, hearing shouts. As he reached the end of the first block someone had gotten to a fire bell and was ringing it madly.

A grinning Lem joined Marty and Luke in front of the bank. But as they started up the steps to the door, a half dozen people rushed out as they heard the alarm. Several tellers were among them.

As they went through the door, guns drawn, the two guards began to yell at one of the bank officers. Marty and Luke fired and the guards went down, sprawling on the floor. The bank officer shouted something and ran into his office, slamming the door.

"Lem, get the money!" Marty snapped. "By the door!" He and Luke rushed to the back where the safe was standing open. They frantically filled the four sacks they had brought.

The bank officer opened the office door, and a pistol poked out. Lem sent four shots slamming through the thin wood.

Marty growled. "That's all—let's go!"

Lem grabbed a sack, and they ran out to the horses. The bell was still ringing, and a crowd of people had gathered in the street before the hotel, which was burning fiercely. A fire engine had arrived, and men pumped frantically, throwing a stream of water on the flames. Marty saw a dozen white faces turn toward them as they mounted the horses.

Luke led out, and a few people along the street shouted, but no one attempted to stop them.

Laredo and Pete arrived in Peryton and went at once to call on Dr. Shipley, asking about Mrs. Moody.

"She died of cancer."

"Was Matt Moody at the funeral?"

"Yes, he was. But I can't tell you where he is now."

"Was he alone?"

"He appeared to be."

Pete asked, "You aren't defending him?"

Shipley sighed deeply. "I'm deathly afraid of him. I admit it. But I know nothing of his movements."

"Thanks, doctor."

They took the road that led past the Moody farm and were surprised to see workers burning piles of brush in the fields. Beyond them cattle were grazing. The house, what they could see of it, seemed closed up, no smoke coming from the chimney. There were mules in the corral near the barn, but it was impossible to tell if Moody was in the house or not.

They rode into the fields, and a worker told them that the Moody's hired man, Sam, lived in the barn and looked after the place. It was Sam who paid them each week. Where he got the money, no one knew. "He done that even when Miz Moody was alive," a man told them.

None of the workers knew anything about Matt. They had not seen him since the funeral.

There was probably no point in talking to Sam. His answers would doubtless be biased and, Pete thought, he probably knew no more than the field hands. It was unlikely that Matt Moody would confide in him.

They were at another dead end.

Until they read the newspapers. There had been a bank holdup at Medina. Two bank guards and a bank official had been killed and some forty thousand dollars taken.

None of the descriptions of the robbers fit Matt Moody, but several described Marty Nevers. There had been two others with him. There had also been a hotel fire that had broken out at the same time as the bank robbery, leading the sheriff to conjecture that the fire had been deliberately set to take attention from the bank.

"It sounds like a Moody job," Laredo said.

"But without Moody. Maybe he was at the funeral then."

"Let's go talk to the sheriff in Medina."

They first wired John Fleming, telling him where they were. Fleming replied that he was very surprised that the hundreds of posters with T.R.'s picture on them had turned up no one grabbing at the reward. Not a single person had come forward. Was it possible T.R. was no longer among the living? Or was it possible that Matt Moody had outsmarted them all?

Questions without answers.

Laredo shook his head as they left the telegraph office. "His actions don't seem to bear it out—that he's outsmarted everyone."

"That's true. He went chasing after T.R., and T.R. barely got away, with or without the money." Pete lit a brown cigarette. "What in hell happened to that money?"

"Maybe Moody *has* outsmarted us . . . and his gang. Maybe he didn't hide the money originally where he said he did."

"You mean he's been playacting ever since?"

"Why not? There're big stakes—one hundred and fifty thousand of them."

Pete was silent for several moments. "What if a third party got it?"

"You said a third party couldn't have."

Pete grinned. "Circumstances change one's mind sometimes. I admit the third-party theory is not very plausible. But I like the idea that Matt Moody has it—it's very devious."

"Maybe too devious for him?"

Pete nodded. "Maybe. But if he has it, then it's probably still on the Moody farm—somewhere. He grew up there, as far as we know, so he probably knows a hundred excellent hiding places."

Laredo pushed up his hat with a finger. "You know, that would explain why T.R. hasn't shown up somewhere, spending the money. He doesn't have it!"

"This entire thing is getting too complicated, as John said. There're too many maybes." Pete shook his head and looked toward the setting sun. "But where would it be on the Moody farm? Just about every inch has been cleared and burned or plowed under. T.R. *must* have taken the money with him."

"Then why hasn't anyone seen him? Why isn't he spending it? His picture is everywhere."

"That's it. He's holed up in a nice safe place, waiting till all the noise dies down. Probably he's seen some of the posters, and he's waiting till they get ripped down or other posters put up over them."

Laredo made a wry face. "But criminal types like T.R. don't have that much patience, do they?"

"That's a good point." Pete sighed deeply. "Where the hell is that money?"

When they counted the Medina State Bank money on the kitchen table in the Moody farmhouse, they had thirty-five thousand, four hundred and nine dollars. Matt rubbed his hands together, very pleased. He hadn't expected more than twenty thousand, he said.

They divided it carefully, four ways—less than nine thousand each, but a good start on a nest egg. *Another* start, Matt said sourly.

After this, he told them, they would divvy the money up after every job. It had been a terrible mistake not to with the reservation agent's money. It had proved too much of a temptation.

But now, what about the next job? They had the summer before them. They ought to do three or four more banks before the first snow flurries.

Luke had never had so much money before in his life and wanted to celebrate. He had a woman in Camp Hill, he said, and would like to return there for a while if no one had any objections.

Matt shrugged. They were three now and didn't really need Luke. He let the other go.

Matt was amused at the diversion—burning down the hotel in Medina. Maybe they ought to burn down a hotel in every town that had a good bank prospect. But Marty argued that it wouldn't take long for people to get on to the dodge and run to the nearest bank as soon as a fire started.

"Could be any bank," Matt said. "So we pick towns with more than one bank."

"What about cattle?" Lem asked.

They looked at him. Marty said, "Steal a herd, you mean?"

"Why not? There's as much money in cows as in robbing banks."

"He's right," Marty agreed. "And less risk."

Matt glumly lit a cigar. "Maybe. But a hell of a lot more work. You go in and out of a bank in five minutes. With a herd you got to wet-nurse 'em for a hunnerd miles."

"It ain't that bad."

"Well, what about Fairview?" Marty said. "We could look it over."

"Yeh, good idea," Matt said. "And if we see some cows along the way . . ." He slapped Lem's back.

T.R. forced himself to stay away from the farm for several days. The workers would have the land cleared soon and would probably pack up and skedaddle—maybe with the damned dogs.

He made a journey south to the first town, Biggars, and had a shave and haircut, then a soak in a tin tub. He spent time in one of the saloons and dallied with some of the painted girls. One of them said she thought he reminded her of someone, she couldn't remember who.

He saw only one poster and ripped it down when no one was looking.

He bought supplies, piled them in a grain sack, and rode back to his niche in the rocks. When he crept close to the barbed-wire fence, newly put up, he discovered men were bringing in cattle. Others were continuing the wire around the property.

And worse than all of that, they were living in the old shack, which had been converted into a bunkhouse. There was no way he could even get close to it. The hired man, Sam, knew him by sight, of course. If he suddenly turned up, Sam would certainly relay the information to Matt, and Matt wouldn't wonder for long why he was on the farm. Matt would soon realize the money was still there, hidden somewhere, and sooner or later he would find it.

No, he had to keep out of sight.

It was frustrating, but he was helpless. And he was getting damned tired of living like a hunted animal—when a fortune was almost within reach.

Chapter Fifteen

THE law in Medina was a deputy sheriff named Hank Vickers, an old-timer who scanned their credentials. "What you want to know?"

"About the bank robbery," Laredo said. "We think it might have been the Matt Moody gang."

"Think so m'self." Vickers fished in his desk and found a cigar. "But Matt wasn't with them."

"You're sure?"

"Yep. Got descriptions of all three. One was sure as hell Marty Nevers. He been ridin' with Matt for years. 'Nother was Lem Bowman. He been with Matt a long time, too. We don't have no picture of him, but we know what he looks like. The third one we ain't sure of. It wasn't Toby Rogers, that's for damn sure. We think they picked this new guy up to do the job with them." He lit the cigar.

"The papers suspicion they burned down the hotel."

Vickers sighed deeply. "The hotel and two stores. I can't prove they done it, but like the paper says, it's suspicious as hell, it coming at exactly the same time as the robbery. And we know them three stayed in the hotel."

Pete said, "You went after them, of course."

The deputy nodded. "We follered 'em as far south as the stage road—and lost 'em." He pointed out the route on a map that was tacked to an office wall.

When they went out to the horses Laredo said, "Do you suppose they went back to the farm?"

"They might have, if they left Matt there."

"Or they could have met him somewhere."

Pete shrugged. "We know he went to his mother's funeral. That took place at about the same time as the robbery. I say they all met again at the farm."

Laredo nodded. "Then what did they do?"

Pete looked at him sidelong. "They did what all bank robbers do—they planned another robbery."

"Or they went to spend the money."

"Yes, or that."

They headed for the farm again.

Bob Flagg, drunk as a trooper, tried to slap water on his face from the horse trough in front of the general store—and fell in. Howie helped pull him out. "You damn fool."

It sobered Flagg a bit. He slogged back to the hotel for dry clothes. He owned another shirt and a pair of jeans. Howie went with him, having no other place to go. When they got in the room, Howie pointed out that neither of them had more than a dollar to his name.

"We ain't going to eat very long on nothing."

"You got a gun?" Flagg demanded.

"Course I got a gun. You want to hold up somebody?"

"Ain't that the quickest way to get money?"

Howie shrugged his thin shoulders. "When we going to do it?"

"Why not tonight? Soon's it gets good and dark."

"Then what?"

"Then we git the hell outa town."

"Where to?"

Flagg pulled his revolver and looked at the brass. "The next town is Fairview. What about that?"

"All right with me."

Fairview, named by an early settler with a vast imagination, was on the high plains, a dusty, windy town on a railroad spur line. It was a cattle shipping point and was very busy twice a year. In between it drowsed, waking briefly when a train pulled in, which was only once a month.

A few small herds and some horses changed hands during the year, which generally kept the corrals and stablemen occupied.

Matt was not impressed with what he saw. The town looked poor and seedy. "The damn bank'll have forty dollars in the safe this time of year. We ought to wait till fall."

"But we're here now."

Lem said, "Maybe we can steal a herd and bring 'em here."

Marty mused. "What about the express office?"

Matt stared at him. "The express office?"

"It should have a few thousand. Maybe as much as five."

Matt shook his head. "I don't like the getaway from here. Country's too goddamn flat."

"We can do it smart," Marty said.

"What you mean?"

"I mean we hide spare horses a few miles outa town, so we gallop out and change horses, and the posse'll have to give it up. We done that before."

Matt nodded. "That's right. It's a good idee. But first we got to steal three horses."

They went out to look at the bank and at the express office. One at a time they drifted in and out. When they met later they discussed their findings.

The bank had only one guard on the main floor. Probably the tellers weren't armed; neither of them looked like he knew one end of a gun from the other. The express office was in the brown railroad depot building. The three men they saw inside were all wearing pistols, and there were five shotguns in a rack on the wall. Also, two doors were standing open, and there was no way to know if there were more armed men there, too.

"Let's hit the bank," Marty said.

"There's horses in a pen behind the livery," Lem said. "I'll walk down there tonight and take another look."

"Go alone," Matt told him. "Playact you're a drifter."

Lem rolled his eyes. "I was thinkin' of takin' along a drum."

Matt growled at him and flopped on the bed.

They ate supper in a grub shop. Lem made his walk late at night and returned to say there were fourteen horses in the pen. "It's Number Eight smooth wire. A pair of cutters is all we need."

"Get 'em tomorrow," Matt said. "We'll take the horses out in the sticks and hit the bank the next morning."

"Suits me." Marty agreed, and Lem nodded.

In the morning Lem bought a pair of cutters, then he and Marty bought food, dividing it into three gunny sacks, telling the store owner they were pointing north.

That night, late, they cut the pen wire, selected three horses, and Lem and Marty led them south. They picketed the horses in a lonely dry wash where clumps of willows grew high. It took the entire night to do it, and they got back in the gray predawn, satisfied that no one had seen them come or go.

The main street of Fairview led back from the railroad at right angles, not parallel with it. A blacksmith shop and a cobbler stood near the depot on a weedy road that wandered to the cattle pens. The only bank was in the center of town, a narrow building crowded between a millinery shop and a hardware store. The boardwalk was only a step above the rutted street in most places, shaded by the usual unpainted wooden awnings.

A small sign on the front door of the bank stated that it was open from 10 A.M. until 3 P.M. Matt, Lem, and Marty got down in front as a boy propped the bank door open. Three people were waiting to get in, and Matt politely let them go ahead.

When the three customers emerged a few minutes later, he and Marty walked in while Lem leaned against the door, glancing up and down the empty street. Then he removed the prop, closed the door, and bolted it.

Marty herded the two tellers and a bank officer into one of the tiny rooms, pushing with the muzzle of his revolver. "Stay still, and you won't get hurt."

A second bank officer was surprised as he opened the safe for the morning's business. He stared into the muzzle of Matt's pistol and slowly got to his feet, arms raised. Matt shoved him into the room with the others and slammed the door.

They filled the sacks they had brought, and Matt tossed one to Lem. "Let's go—open the door."

Lem pulled the bolt back and pushed the door open as Matt and Marty rushed from the back. Lem started out to the horses as a shot was fired from the rear of the bank. The bullet smashed into the wall over his head.

Matt turned and fired three shots wildly, as fast as he could work the hammer. He yelled, "Come on!" and dashed out to the street.

A second shot brought Marty down. He was behind Matt, who did not notice his friend had been hit. Matt and Lem piled on the horses, and Lem yelled, "Where's Marty?"

They milled in the street for a few moments, but Marty did not appear. Men spilled from the stores behind them, and several shots were fired. Someone shouted that the bank was being held up.

Matt growled and put spurs to his horse. He and Lem fled down the street and into the prairie.

Marty had been hit just below the left knee. He left the money sack and tried to crawl to the front door but someone put a pistol in his back and said, "Stay put, mister."

They took his gun and tied his hands, rolling him onto his back, and a boy ran for the law. Marty swore and gritted his teeth as the pain began to spread. They had him for sure this time.

The town marshal appeared, then a doctor with his black bag. The doctor cut off his pants leg and clucked over the wound. Marty passed out as the other worked on him.

When he came to he was in a jail cell, bandaged and

splinted. The doc had left him laudanum for pain. He took some at once.

He lay on the bed for several hours, and no one came near him. Then the marshal entered and sat on the end of the cot. "Who was them others?"

"I just met 'em two days ago. All's I know is one is named Terry and one Jack."

"What's your name?"

"Henry Sims. I never done this before. I was down on my luck. . . ."

"Where'd they go?"

"I dunno. We was going to split up soon's we got out of town."

The marshal got up, and the doctor came into the cell.

Marty asked, "How bad is it?"

"You're going to limp the rest of your days. The bone will knit, but it's partly shattered. Try not to move it."

Marty nodded, and the doctor left, saying he would be back in a day or two.

Marty was locked in a dim room with two other cells, both empty. He tried to relax on the hard bunk with the pain throbbing, wondering how long it would take the marshal to find out who he had in his jail.

Matt and Lem reined in a few miles outside of town and looked back. Lem said, "Marty must of got hit bad."

"Did you see 'im go down?"

"No."

Matt swore. They could see a half dozen men streaming out of town toward them. He hugged the money bag and spurred the horse.

They galloped the animals hard, and both were heaving when they reached the dry wash. In moments they had pulled off saddles, bridles, and blankets and swapped, mounting the fresh animals.

They did not see the posse again. Matt led in a wide circle over the sod. Unless one of the posse were an expert tracker, a very unlikely thing, they would give up.

Long after dark they approached the town again from the opposite direction. Matt's picture was well posted, so Lem went in alone, walking his horse like an ordinary drifter. He sat in a saloon and listened to the gossip. It was all about the robbery. Apparently no one in the room had actually seen it, but everyone knew that one of the robbers was in the town jail, shot in the leg. No one mentioned Matt Moody. That meant Marty had not yet been identified.

Lem wandered out and rejoined Matt. "Marty's in the jailhouse with a shot-up leg. But they don't know who he is."

"That's good." Matt pulled at his chin. "Tomorra you go in and have a look at that jail."

"All right, but we can't move 'im with a busted-up leg."

Matt growled about it, but he knew Lem was right. They would have to wait until Marty could travel.

He had counted the money in the two bags while Lem had been in the town. They had only three thousand and seventy-two dollars.

And Marty in the carcel, shot up.

Chapter Sixteen

Laredo and Pete halted a distance from the Moody farmhouse and studied it through binoculars. There was no smoke from the chimney; no one seemed to be about.

But there were cattle in the far fields, and a few men were working, moving around. There was a small pole corral newly built beside the old shack; it held half a dozen horses.

Pete said, "It looks like they're turning the farm into a ranch. Probably with stolen money."

"Guilty till proven innocent."

"Well, how else does Moody get money? Unless his mother had money in the mattress."

Laredo said, "If she had money, he gave it to her. Is Matt Moody here?"

"No telling. But he's probably out robbing banks to get more money to buy cattle."

"Why doesn't he just steal them?"

"Because there's brands on them that can be traced."

Laredo chuckled. "If he's out robbing banks to get money to buy cattle, doesn't that prove he hasn't got the reservation money?"

"It's suspiciously like it, yes."

"Then we're back to T.R."

"Unless Matt is more devious than we think."

Pete rolled a cigarette. "Going into a bank to rob it is dangerous. If he had the reservation money would he do it?"

"He's an outlaw. He's been doing it for years. He probably never gives the danger a thought."

Pete licked the paper flap. "T.R. is a mystery. There's a thousand posters out for him, and no one has seen him. Is he holed up with the money?"

"Didn't we agree that it had to be T.R. or Matt Moody?"

"I vote for T.R. The last time anybody ever heard of the money he had it—as far as we know."

"As far as we know."

Pete lit the cigarette. "A little while ago you said he didn't have the patience to wait it out. Have you changed your mind?"

"A while ago you mentioned how circumstances change things."

Pete chuckled, blowing smoke. "It goes round and round, and always comes back to: Where the hell is the money?"

"T.R.'s probably got it, holed up with it, patience or no patience. What else makes any sense?"

Pete puffed and looked at the glowing end of the cigarette. "I'm afraid so." He glanced at Laredo. "So where is he?"

The doctor came in two days to look at the wound. He removed the bandages, applied a compound, and rebandaged the leg. He was a young man, recently out of medical school, he told Marty. He was very concerned about his patient, bank robber or not. His name was Hiram Watts, and he was very serious in manner. He had just taken over the practice of a much older man who wanted to retire. Watts was now the only physician in the area.

The leg must be kept immobile or dire things could result, he warned. He might even lose the leg. Marshal Evans wanted to send Marty in the prisoner wagon to the county seat for trial, but Dr. Watts forbade it—for the time being.

The local photographer came into the cell to take Marty's picture, at Evans's order. But Marty managed to twist his face slightly, so that when the picture was developed it did not look a great deal like him. Marshal Evans was angry, but a second picture turned out no better, and he gave it up.

He was entered in the record as Henry Sims; he had nothing on his person to contradict or prove it. The local newspaper mentioned Henry Sims in passing when the robbery was detailed. The reporter printed what Sims told him, that he had been down on his luck and had happened to meet the two men, Terry and Jack, and had gone along with them. It was his first foray into crime, and he was sorry for it. He said that when his mother heard about it, she would be very sad.

Lem and Matt camped west of the town, and Lem went in each night to sit and listen to the talk, but he learned nothing new. The newspaper, when it came out, said very little either.

Lem reported to Matt that the jail was a cracker box, used mostly for weekend drunks. They ought to be able to break Marty out easily when he was fit to travel.

On Saturday night, when cowhands roared in from several nearby ranches, Lem bought a small bottle of whiskey, drank some of it late in the evening, poured the rest of it over his clothes, and fell across the boardwalk nearly in front of the jail.

He was quickly taken inside and dumped on a cot. In the course of the night, a half dozen others met the same fate.

The cell was next to Marty's, and when they could talk they put their heads together at the bars. He was well cared for, Marty said, but in a week or so they would take him in a wagon to the county seat to stand trial. He could expect to be sent to Logansville Territorial Prison forever.

"Get me outa here," he said to Lem. "When they take me for trial they'll find out who I am . . . and they might hang me. Either that or I'll spend the rest of my life in the damned prison."

"We'll get you out. It just depends on when you can git on a horse."

"I'll keep after the doc. He's a young kid and don't know nothing."

Marshal Evans turned Lem out on Monday morning, and

Lem joined Matt immediately. "I could have smuggled a couple of derringers into jail," he said. "They don't hardly search the drunks at all."

"When the time comes, that's the way we'll do it then," Matt replied. "You and him inside and me outside. I'll have three horses waiting."

Bob Flagg and Howie arrived in Fairview late at night and spent the rest of it in the stable with the horses.

Howie had bummed a few dollars from a friend, so they had breakfast and heard about the bank robbery as they ate. Someone had beaten them to the safe, but one of the robbers was in the clink with a busted-up leg. Somebody named Henry Sims. No one had ever heard of him.

They stood in the street, and Flagg said, "No chance at the bank now. We got to move on."

"What about the railroad?" Howie nodded toward the depot.

Flagg glared at the other. "The railroad! You ever robbed a train?"

"Well, no . . . but they carry money in the express cars."

"How d'you know that?"

Howie was annoyed. "From readin' the newspapers, for crissakes."

That was so. Flagg had read them, too. He wasn't sure which one was the express car—was it marked? They walked to the depot and looked at the train schedules. The next train to Fairview was three weeks away.

"Three weeks!" Flagg said. "They only run one train a month!"

Howie sighed. "Then we do something else. Maybe we ought to stay with the holdup business."

Flagg nodded. That was probably the best idea. It didn't pay much as a rule, but it would keep them eating. Of course, it would also keep them on the move, to prevent their being recognized by one of the victims.

But there was always the chance that they might get lucky. . . .

The best saloon in town was the American Bar. It was on a corner and had a large hall for dancing where a band played. There was also a stage for performers and plenty of painted women circulating.

They would hang around outside the saloon at night, Flagg said, and watch for prosperous citizens.

They waited till very late, standing in the shadows, eyeing everyone who came out the bat-wing doors. Most were ordinary looking, men who might, with luck, have a dollar left.

But finally a well-dressed man came out. He had a gold chain across his ample middle and was smoking a fat cigar. Flagg nudged Howie.

They followed the prospective victim a short distance, then Flagg moved in close and put a gun in the man's back. "Stop right here."

The man halted in astonishment as Howie circled around in front. "Don't move!" Flagg growled, pushing with the gun muzzle, clicking back the hammer, *click-clack*—to increase the effect. The victim gulped as Howie lifted the man's watch and wallet.

Then Flagg commanded: "Run!" The man shambled away.

As they turned back toward the saloon, another man came out and stared at them. Lem Bowman gasped and grabbed at his Colt. "Flagg! You son of a bitch!" He fired twice as Flagg screamed and ran.

He knocked Howie out of the way and ran down the street, passing his recent victim as Lem fired four more times. Flagg disappeared in the dark as men came spilling from the saloons asking what was happening.

Lem got on his horse and loped after Flagg but did not find him.

John Fleming had suggested that Matt Moody and his accomplices could not long stay out of banks, since that was their occupation, so Laredo and Pete watched the newspapers for clues.

111

Two robberies were reported within days of each other, but their locations were too far apart for them to have been the work of the same gang. One of the banks was in Tellis, the other in Fairview. Tellis was much closer, so they rode there at once.

The bank was the Tellis County National, and two bandits had gotten away with a total of three thousand dollars, in round numbers. Not knowing better, they had come on a day when most of the bank's cash had just been delivered to the parent bank in Janisburg.

"They were unlucky," the bank manager told them happily. "If they'd come the day before . . ."

"Only two men?" Pete asked.

"Two were all we saw." He described them, and neither had been Matt Moody. One might have been Nevers. And there might have been a man outside with the horses.

The manager said, "We all had the same impression, that they didn't act as if they'd done this before. They were nervous and edgy, ready to shoot. So none of us gave them any argument."

"Then it wasn't the Moody gang," Pete said definitely.

Laredo agreed. "We're in the wrong town."

But Fairview was probably the wrong town, also. The newspaper item said one of the outlaws had been captured and his name was Henry Sims. So the Fairview robbery was probably the work of another gang, too.

But it was their only lead.

It was a long journey across country to the town on the high plains. They arrived in the middle of the day and went at once to call on the town marshall. He was a short, dumpy man, unshaven and shabby, looking more like a sharecropper than a lawman. He pored over their credentials, never having seen anything like them before.

He looked at them as if they'd come from the moon. "You all federal men! What you want wi' me?"

"We want to ask you about the bank robbery."

"Oh. Izzat all? We got one of 'em in jail here. He's a little shot-up . . ."

"What's he told you?"

"Not a damn thing. Said he was a drifter down on 'is luck. Said he never done nothing like that before. Didn't know the other two gents."

Pete said, "Let's have a look at him."

The marshal nodded. "Name's Henry Sims." He took a large wooden paddle off a nail. It had an iron key ring and several keys attached. He unlocked the heavy, iron-bound jail door and stood aside.

Laredo and Pete walked to the bars and looked at Marty Nevers. He was lying on a bunk bed, well bandaged. He stared back at them, his face stubbled with beard.

Without a word Laredo turned; he and Pete went back into the office and closed the heavy door. When the marshal had locked the door Laredo said, "His name isn't Sims."

The marshal was astonished. "You know 'im?"

"That's Marty Nevers. One of Matt Moody's gang."

The other's jaw dropped. "Moody!"

Pete said, "Don't you have a poster on Nevers?"

"I—I—I never thought . . . Jesus! Marty Nevers! Are you all sure?"

"Certainly we're sure." Laredo showed him the photo of Nevers. "Do you have any deputies?"

"Why?"

"Because Matt will probably try to get Nevers out. Can he be moved?"

"The doc says no, not for a week or two." The marshal was visibly shaken by the news that he had a notorious outlaw in his cracker-box jail. He was almost wringing his hands. He said, "I got two boys who help out sometimes, but they ain't deputies. This here's the biggest crime we ever had in town."

Laredo said, "If I were you, I'd deputize half a dozen men and keep this office forted up—or you're going to lose Nevers."

The marshal looked from one to the other of them. "You figger it's that bad?"

Pete said, "Matt Moody is a killer. He'll stop at nothing to get him out."

The shabby man sat at his desk like a sack of potatoes, all the color drained from his face. "W-will he come in here? The doc says he can't be moved."

"He probably means on a horse. Moody will come with a buckboard. D'you know men you can deputize?"

"Will he come in the daytime?"

Laredo shook his head. "Probably at night."

"Y-yes, I think so. . . ."

"Then you'd best get about it." Laredo smiled reassuringly. "We'll stay here while you go after them."

The marshal nodded and got up slowly. He took a deep breath, glanced at them, and went out.

Pete said when he was gone, "Do you suppose he was voted into office?"

Laredo chuckled. "Probably appointed by a relative. I suppose we can assume that Matt Moody knows Nevers is here."

"We'd be smart to assume it. Maybe I'd better go wire the U.S. Marshal's office that Nevers is here in jail."

"Wire John Fleming, too."

Pete went to the door. "You know, they could put Nevers on a cot and carry it to a house nearby—after dark, of course."

"But if someone saw it or if Moody found out, a house wouldn't be as good a fort as this jail."

"I suppose not." Pete left.

Chapter Seventeen

Pete returned half an hour later. The marshal's office had merely acknowledged the wire. Fleming had replied that he would bring pressure to bear on that marshal to take Nevers into custody and transport him to the nearest federal judge for trial. The government had a long list of crimes to charge him with.

The dumpy town marshal was away nearly two hours, and when he returned he was tired and irritable. No one he'd approached would volunteer. But he had talked to several of the town council, and they had agreed to put up money to pay for guards for the jail.

Bob Flagg squeezed under the boardwalk and lay motionless as Lem Bowman galloped by. Then he crawled out and ran to meet Howic, who had their horses. They crossed the railroad tracks and headed east, two shadows in the night.

Flagg's heart was still pounding. Lem would have killed him! And if Lem was in the town, did that mean that Matt was alive? Jesus, Matt alive! He'd seen him dead on the floor. Well, he *thought* he'd seen Matt dead. . . . Flagg shuddered. He'd better put as much distance between them as possible—just in case. If he came across a telegraph office, he would wire the law, telling them where Moody was to be found.

* * *

When Lem told Matt he had seen Bob Flagg, shot at him in fact, Matt was raging. "That son of a bitch that close? How come you let him get away?"

"They was a thousand places to hide—it was dark, for crissakes."

Matt wanted to ride into town to look for him, but Lem finally talked him out of it, saying Flagg was doubtless on his way somewhere else, knowing Matt would kill him on sight.

Lem said, "No sense in the law grabbing you over a skunk like Flagg."

Lem reported that the town had a sack of beans for a marshal and a grubby little jail. A bar idler had told him that the marshal was a toady, appointed by some of the merchants who used him for their own ends. He had no deputies, and the jail was only used for occasional drunks. The railroad, when it came into town once a month, had its own guards.

He had also learned that an important prisoner like Marty would have to be taken to court at the county seat. No one knew when that would be.

Lem said, "But it won't be till the doc says Marty can go. Maybe a week or so."

"He's only got a busted-up leg," Matt protested.

"Yeah, but the prisoner wagon ain't got any springs. It'll jolt that leg and maybe send bones through the skin and start the bleedin'."

Matt grunted, and Lem continued: "They don't want him to bleed t'death, they want to hang him."

"Stop talkin' like that. Nobody's goin' to hang him."

Lem shrugged.

The following week Lem bought another bottle of whiskey, doused himself with it, and was hauled into jail with other prisoners who really were drunk. Late at night he talked with Marty when the others were snoring.

The doctor had been to see him several times, Marty said. The leg was knitting nicely, and he thought he would be moved soon.

"I hear they going to hang me at the county seat."

"They won't. We going to get you out," Lem promised. "You be ready." He slipped Marty the two derringers he had brought.

Marty's eyes lighted up at the sight of them. Two over-and-under Remingtons, .41-caliber. He put them away quickly, grinning like a kid with a stolen pie. Now he had four shots, two in each hand.

Lem and Matt talked it over. Marty would probably be able to stick on a horse in a few days—Marty thought so. They had planned to hit the prisoner wagon, but why not the jail?

Matt said, "They'll expect us to go after the wagon. And they won't expect Marty to have them derringers in the jail. Besides, they might search him good before they put him in the wagon."

"That's right."

"So how about tomorra night?"

Lem nodded. "All right. How you want to do it?"

"I'll be the drunk. You hold me up, and we'll go into the jail office. You tell whoever's there that you want me tossed in one of the cells."

"That's good. Ought to work slick as bear grease."

They waited till the town was quiet, then tied three horses near the jail office. Then Matt leaned heavily on Lem and began grumbling and talking, staggering and swearing at Lem as they approached the jail. Lem pounded on the locked door.

A voice answered, "What you want?"

"Got a damn drunk here," Lem yelled. "Lemme in, dammit!"

A curious face appeared at the door and looked at them, and Lem pushed in. There was one man behind the marshal's desk and another standing in the jail door with a shotgun. Matt broke away from Lem and began shooting. Lem fired at the two men in front of him, seeing both topple.

117

The man with the shotgun ran into the jail, and there were two shots fired close together. When Lem looked into the cell area the man with the shotgun was sprawled on the floor, and Marty was grinning at him.

"Get the goddamn keys." He put the derringers into his pockets.

Laredo and Pete, several blocks from the jail, were awakened late at night by the shooting. Laredo sat up in bed. Were drunken cowhands letting off steam? He looked at his watch. Midnight.

Across the room Pete said, "It's Wednesday—you figure that's in a saloon?"

"If it's not"—Laredo swung out of bed and grabbed his pants—"it's the jail."

Pete growled under his breath.

They dressed and hurried out to the street. No one was about. The street was dark as they ran toward the jail. Others showed themselves as they approached. A man said, "It come from the jailhouse."

There was a lantern glowing in the jail office, and the door was standing open. Laredo entered cautiously, pistol drawn . . . and swore.

There were two bodies on the floor and another in the cell area. Marty Nevers's cell door was standing open, and he was gone.

Someone said, "They busted him out."

The marshal came running in. He had been sleeping and was only half-dressed. He made a face, seeing the bodies. "What happened?"

Laredo's tone was icy. "You didn't take Matt Moody seriously, friend." He and Pete walked out.

In the street, Pete rolled a cigarette. "Somehow they got one of the guards to open the front door. Then they just shot them all down."

Laredo shook his head sadly.

They went to call on Dr. Watts in the morning. He was attending a birthing in a woman's home, Mrs. Watts said.

They waited an hour for him to return, and when he got there, he shook his head at Laredo's question.

"He is healing quickly. I doubt if he can ride as he used to, but he could manage pretty well, favoring the leg."

"Can he walk on it?"

"No, definitely not. Not for about a month. But he could get around on crutches. He's not a weakling by any stretch."

"Will he need to have it looked at by another doctor?"

"Need?" Watts smiled. "Maybe not need, but I can tell you if it were my leg, I'd want a physician to look at it now and then."

They thanked him and left, going at once to the telegraph office. They wired John Fleming, telling him what had happened, admitting they had no clue to Matt Moody's whereabouts.

Fleming replied that the Moody farm might be a suggestion. Since Marty Nevers was hurt and the local law in Peryton was in Moody's pocket, he would certainly consider himself safe there.

However, if they discovered that Moody and the others were there, the United States Marshal in Ettinger must be notified. Fleming gave them strict orders not to attempt Moody's capture if he were with any of the gang. His superiors had changed their opinions and now wanted Moody alive, if possible. And he, Fleming, did not want *them* dead.

Fleming went on to explain that Moody *might* know where the reservation money was hidden and that that information might die with him. It was a chance Fleming did not want to take. Of course, many times Moody had sworn he would not be taken alive—he feared being hanged. Fleming felt that if the U.S. Marshal surrounded the farm with enough men, Moody would have to surrender, oath or no oath.

It was the most restrictive order Fleming had ever issued to them, but Matt Moody's reputation as a vicious killer was doubtless in the forefront of Fleming's mind. He well knew that anything could happen in a gunfight.

They returned to Peryton and got down in front of Dr. Shipley's home late at night, when they were certain he would

119

be alone. In a gray dressing gown, he let them in. "What is it?"

"Have you seen Matt Moody or treated Marty Nevers?"

"No, I haven't seen either. What's wrong with Nevers?"

"A gunshot wound in the leg."

"I've heard nothing about them for weeks."

When they rode by the Moody farmhouse it looked deserted.

Pete said gloomily, "They're probably in Kansas City."

Chapter Eighteen

T.R. was completely frustrated. The dogs were still on the farm, roaming at large, and men were living in the shack-turned-bunkhouse. There was no way he could get close to it, short of killing the dogs. And to do that he would have to shoot them, which he dared not do.

There were times when he thought of walking into the shack late at night and shooting the men and the dogs—to end his frustration. But of course that had its dangers, too. The men certainly were armed, and he might easily be killed in the fracas.

The possibility that Matt Moody had already discovered the money sack on the roof of the shack ate at him. If he had found it, Matt would never advertise it.

T.R. knew that the only way he could know for sure was to climb onto the roof. And it seemed that was impossible.

How long could he live in his rocky cave, waiting for the moment to come when he could get his hands on the money? At times he felt himself going mad. Nothing had ever been so completely frustrating. The fortune was so close—and so damned far! He spent long hours dreaming of how he would spend it, and the dreams almost seemed to become reality. Half-awake, he could feel the silkiness of a girl's hands, the taste of fine liquor and rich food—and then he would waken to the cave and vittles from a grain sack.

Living as he did, things such as shaving became a bother.

He let his facial hair grow. He bought a pair of scissors and kept the beard trimmed a reasonable length with the aid of a little pocket mirror.

The beard changed his appearance completely.

One of the field hands had reported to Sam, the hired man, that he had seen a furtive figure skulking about in the early evenings, probably someone looking to steal tools or anything he could sell in town.

It was the reason Sam had bought the dogs.

The mysterious figure had been seen since, but never close by, and nothing was reported missing. So Sam did not bother Mr. Matt with it. There were a lot of people in the world who were not right in the head, Sam knew. This skulker might well be one of them. The dogs were keeping him away.

It was a long journey to the farm for Marty Nevers. The wound hurt abominably, despite the laudanum he took, which made him feel tired and drowsy.

He was constantly under tension, having to hold the leg at an unnatural angle in the saddle, so he tired easily and had to call a halt every few miles. Matt growled about it, saying it made the journey three times as long as it should be.

When they finally arrived at the farm, Marty flopped on one of the bunks in the barn and slept the clock round. There was some bleeding from the wound; the bandages were soaked. He wanted to get the doctor in Peryton to look at the leg, but Matt snarled that he wanted no one to know where they were.

"You forgot how your own wound was, dammit!"

"No, I haven't. But you ain't in bad shape. Them splints hold the bones straight. All's you got is a little cut bleedin'." Matt strode out of the barn.

Sam had some papers and bills of sale, reporting to Matt that they now had more than eight hundred head of cattle in the fields.

"The grass ain't goin' to hold out much longer, Mr. Matt. 'Nother week'n we has to haul in feed."

"Then we'll drive 'em to market."

Matt decided they would go to Sidley on the railroad, a journey of some two hundred miles as the crow flew. He and Lem would trail them; Marty and Sam would stay behind.

Sam built a crude chute, and they spent several days shoving the cattle into it, one at a time, slash-branding them for the trip. The bulls would be left behind, along with young calves, cows, and most of the yearlings. The two cowhands, both very young, who were living in the shack-bunkhouse, stayed behind also to look after what was left of the herd and to continue stringing and mending fences.

Matt and Lem left with the herd early one morning, pointing northeast. They had a vague idea where Sidley was and figured to hit the tracks and follow them into the town. They took along three mules with supplies on pack trees.

Matt told Marty, "We prob'ly be gone most of a month. You'll be up an' around time we gets back."

"I hope to hell I will be."

"Get Sam to make you some crutches."

"I will."

Matt waved and went out.

From a distance T.R. watched the herd and riders depart, too far away to tell who they were. They headed northeastward, so they were making for one of the towns along the railroad.

He smiled broadly, thinking that now he had a chance. But when he moved to the barbed-wire fence that night, the dogs were still prowling, and there was a fire in front of the shack. He could see two men there, moving about.

He saw them the next day, working at the fence line. Nothing had changed, except that probably Matt, Lem, and Marty were at the farmhouse. The hired man could not have organized a cattle drive without Matt's permission.

Something *had* changed, it had gotten worse.

He saddled his horse and rode south, feeling very sorry for himself. Biggars hadn't changed since the last time he'd seen it. The town was just as dusty and lonesome. He sat in one of the saloons, and even the company of a buxom whore girl did not cheer him up.

Along the street he saw several posters with his picture on them, but with the beard he knew he looked very different; no one gave him a second glance.

The largest saloon in town was the Trail's End, and he sat in on a quiet game of poker with two others. It was the middle of the week, and the town was sleepy. One of the two was named Brody. He was a farmerish-looking man with spiky yellow hair. He had a house and a privy a few miles out of town, he told them. He had come in for more strychnine.

T.R. asked, "What you want strychnine for?"

"I had me nothing but trouble with coyotes and a few other pests. You can't sit up all night with a shotgun, so I been poisonin' 'em."

"Poison!" T.R. instantly thought of the prowling dogs around the shack.

"I ast Doc Henders," Brody said, "and he told me to get the strychnine. It's a white powder, bitter as hell, so I sew it inside chunks of meat, and them coyotes gulp it down and die like flies."

T.R. smiled. "Where you get strychnine?"

"I get it at Downer's hardware store across the street. Why, you got coyote trouble, too?"

"I sure have," T.R. said.

Later that night in his hotel room he thought about it. If he poisoned the dogs he'd have to be ready to climb onto the roof of the shack at once, because they would know the dogs had been poisoned, and Matt would wonder why.

It didn't matter about the workers living in the shack, because they probably didn't know anything about the money anyway. But Matt would wonder. T.R. well knew how suspicious Matt was. If he poisoned the dogs and still didn't get the money sack off the roof, Matt was likely to institute a search for the poisoner—and turn up his hiding place in the rocks.

So he couldn't poison the dogs until exactly the right time. But he would buy the strychnine and have it ready.

Poison was nice and quiet.

He met Holly the next afternoon. She was dark-haired and not dumpy or fat as many of the girls were, and she reminded him slightly of Doria in Memphis. Of course, she didn't have Doria's fire and liveliness, but there was enough to hold his interest. In her turn she was delighted to find someone in this butt-end-of-creation town who spent money lavishly. She separated him from as many greenbacks as she could, rebuffing all the others who had been sharing her charms for months. She had a dream of going back to Kansas City, and if this drifter stayed around long enough she would earn the fare and a little something besides.

Holly was by far the best-looking girl working the saloon, and T.R.'s moving in, taking up all her time, was not generally approved of. The situation became explosive on Saturday night when a dozen cowhands came in from surrounding ranches, looking for fun, asking for Holly.

She was already busy, they were told. But as the evening wore on and she did not appear as usual, one of the hands went upstairs to investigate. He was young and eager, and when he knocked on her door she shouted, "Go away!"

He knocked again. "Dammit, Holly, what you doing?"

"What the hell you think I'm doing? Go away!"

But he was curious. He opened the door to protest.

T.R. sat up in bed, yanked back the hammer of his Colt, and shot the intruder twice, then once more as he lay on the floor.

Holly said, "Geesis! Didja have to shoot 'im?"

The body lay half in the hall, sprawled in the doorway. T.R. slid out of bed and grabbed his jeans. He yanked them up and shoved into his boots.

The saloon downstairs was suddenly quiet. There were boot heels on the steps.

Holly said, "Dammit, why'd you shoot 'im?"

"Shut up."

"Is he dead?"

"Hell yes, he's dead."

In the hall a man's voice said, "Billy!"

T.R. heard the *click-clack* as the man thumbed the hammer of his revolver. He said, "You—in the room—come out here."

T.R. ducked down low as Holly began to babble in fear. He paid no attention but crept close to the body in the doorway.

The man outside repeated, "You inside there—come on out."

T.R. lunged through the doorway. A tall, rangy man stood five or six feet away with a pistol in his hand. But he did not expect T.R. to appear at that angle. He fired too late. His bullet smashed a lamp in the room. T.R.'s shot doubled him and flung him back. A second shot shattered his head.

T.R. grabbed his shirt and coat. Holly's eyes were huge, her face white as paper as she cowered in the bed. He gave her a brief smile and dashed out, down the hall to the end where there was a window. He yanked it up and stepped out onto the slanting roof. He took a second to close the window. There was no one in the hall—they'd be cautious about going up the stairs, not knowing what awaited them. He heard someone calling out to Billy and to Hank.

He slid down the steep tar-paper roof to the eave. There was nothing but grass and weeds below. He dropped his shirt and coat, scrambled to let himself down easy, holding the eave, then let go. He could hear them hollering inside, and he grinned.

Pulling the shirt over his head, he shoved the tail into his pants and shrugged into the brown coat. Now he could hear them yelling in the saloon. He hoped they'd all tramp up the stairs.

He trotted around the building to the front. The street was dark as he found his horse at the hitch rack. He saw no one as he mounted, but he could hear them upstairs over the saloon. Holly was screaming something as he rode slowly away.

The dumb son of a bitch, Billy, had asked for it. He had sure made a mess of the evening.

Of course, they'd ask Holly what his name was. He'd given her one—what was it? Jim or Bob—he couldn't remember. He'd used a hundred names, riding with Matt Moody.

He was slightly annoyed at having to leave so soon. It had been warm and comfortable in Holly's bed. He hadn't expected to be riding away into the night. And he hadn't had a chance to buy his supplies, or the poison. Damn.

At the end of town he reined in and looked back. The light from the saloon was streaming into the street, and men were running out and climbing on horses. Someone was shouting orders and then, to T.R.'s disgust, they began to gallop toward him! Damn! Somebody must have seen him leave.

Turning the horse, he raked the spurs and rode into the night.

Chapter Nineteen

LAREDO and Pete dismounted in the trees far to the side of the Moody farmhouse. Laredo circled around to the front of the barn as Pete came up quietly to the back.

Someone was inside, humming a song and pounding on something with small, quick strokes. Laredo slipped through the door and stood motionless, his eyes adjusting to the sudden gloom. The hired man, Sam, was at a workbench a dozen feet away; he was straightening nails with a hammer.

Laredo moved toward him and said softly, "Hello, Sam."

The other whirled his eyes round. "Who you?"

"Not an enemy."

Sam seemed to relax. "What you all want, mister?"

"Who's in the house?"

"Nobody. Miz Moody, she died a piece back."

Laredo nodded. "I know that Marty Nevers got shot in Fairview. Is he here?"

"You the law, mister?"

"No."

"Then why you want to know?"

"Marty's inside there, isn't he?"

Sam moved restlessly. "They no way I can tell you nothing. I jus' work here, mister." He reached suddenly for a pistol lying on the bench.

Pete said sharply, "Don't touch it!"

Sam pulled his hand back as if he'd touched a snake. He

looked around in surprise. Pete, with a pistol pointing in his general direction, stood at the end of the bench.

"So Marty *is* in the house," Laredo remarked.

Sam was cowed. "Who you two, anyways?"

Laredo said, "We're looking for Toby Rogers."

Sam snorted. "So ever'body else. He's gone, gone, gone."

"No idea where?"

Sam shook his head and chuckled. "He a dead man, you ast me. You all law men, ain't you?"

Laredo shook his head. He went around Sam, picked up the pistol and unloaded it, tossing the shells onto the bench. Sam watched him calmly. Pete went to the door, glancing outside, and Laredo joined him and laid the pistol on a box. They walked toward the trees.

At the horses Pete said, "We going to round up Marty Nevers?"

Laredo swung into the saddle and looked toward the distant house. "If I thought he knew where the money was, or where T.R. is . . ."

"He doesn't."

"I don't think he does either. If we arrest him we'd have to take him back to Fairview." He squinted at Pete. "That's a long ride."

Pete sighed. "Then let him be. We can wire the marshal to come for him."

Laredo nodded. "Very sensible."

T.R. let the horse have its head, galloping along a strange road in pitch darkness. He had no idea where it led, but it was the wrong direction. As a matter of habit he had intended to circle when he got out of sight of the town and go back north.

But these pursuers were too close behind and probably knew the land. All he could hope would be to outdistance them, then reverse direction.

In an hour he came to a fork in the road and instantly went to the right. It was dark enough so the men behind would have to stop and fashion torches to examine the ground for his tracks. He ought to gain much time on them.

He was in slightly hilly country; the road curved and twisted, staying on a level. He could feel the dark loom of hills on both sides, and it was very still except for the sounds of the horse's hoofs. The air was a little misty, and he could not see the stars.

How long would they chase him? Maybe they were relatives of the two men he had killed. Maybe he'd been hasty, shooting Billy, but the man had no business opening the door that way. The other one, Hank, had given him no option. He'd had to shoot to get out of there.

The road went up the slope of a hill, and at the top he reined in and listened, hearing nothing but a distant owl. He must have gained miles on them. Maybe they'd already turned back. A manhunting party raised on the spur of the moment might not be very tenacious.

But if they were still behind him, his tracks would be clear and fresh in the morning. Nothing he could do about that.

He went on, walking the horse for a half an hour, then loping for a short while, then reining in to dismount and walk beside the horse as the cavalry did on long marches. When he mounted again, he galloped the horse for several miles before reining in to walk once more.

Very gradually the sky lightened and he began to make out the shapes of the hills about him. There was no wind at all, the mist seemed to settle lower, and it was cold; he pulled the coat tighter about his shoulders, wishing he had a poncho.

The sun came out at last, and the mists faded away. When the road rose to the crest of another hill, he looked back again. This time he saw a group of riders strung out along the road, far back. T.R. swore. They were damned tenacious. He had to figure some way to lose them.

When the road crossed a dry wash, he turned into it at once. It was several hundred yards wide, with grass and tall weeds growing in dusty brown clumps and long, curving stretches.

The wash curved away from the road, heading generally northwest. He crossed to the far side, looking for a good spot to climb out. The wash was mostly pebbles and pale sand, very dry. His horse's prints were not as well defined as on the road.

He rode for miles and at last came to a rocky area alongside the wash. He spurred the horse up out of the sand, reined in, and walked back with a broom of weeds and brushed out his tracks as well as he could. If his pursuers were poor trackers he might fool them for a time. It was worth trying.

Mounting again he went west into the low hills, staying off skylines. At midday he ate some of the food in his saddlebags, then turned north. He rode all afternoon, walking the horse, loping, walking again, navigating by the distant hill shapes.

When the sun set he came to a well-traveled road and went northwest. His tracks would be lost among dozens of others. He looked for a place to stay the night and came to a wide arroyo. He turned into it and found a convenient niche a mile from the road. He picketed the horse in a wide patch of grass and curled up in his blankets.

Surely he had lost the pursuers.

But he had not. When he approached the road again next morning, they fired at him. Bullets spanged off the near rocks, and he turned instantly, spurring along the arroyo away from them, swearing aloud. How in hell had they managed to follow him this far?

He'd had a quick glimpse of perhaps seven riders, and they followed him, some shouting directions, firing sporadically. But he gradually drew away from them. His horse had had a good night's rest, and probably they had been riding steadily.

Leaving the arroyo at the first likely spot, he went north, riding hard, doing his best to keep brush and trees, the shoulder of a hill, between him and them.

The next sight he had of them there were only three riders behind him. Probably they had the best mounts.

Three-to-one odds were better than seven-to-one. T.R.

pulled the Winchester from its boot and levered a shell into the chamber. It was time to bite back.

He went up over the slope of a hill and reined in. Jumping down, he ran back to the crest. When the riders appeared, he aimed carefully. The shot knocked the leading man from the saddle.

The others veered away instantly, lying along the animals' backs to make a smaller target. Aiming at the horses, T.R. fired five times, as fast as he could work the lever. He saw one animal stumble, take three or four steps and go to its knees, then roll over and kick a few times. The rider jumped clear.

T.R.'s bullets kicked up dust around him, but he scuttled behind the horse's body and lay still. The third man galloped out of range.

T.R. pushed back from the ridge and ran to his horse, grinning widely. That would stop them for a bit. And it ought to give them an idea of what kind of man they were pursuing. Now they would have to approach every small hill with caution. It would slow them to a walk. If they had any sense they would turn back.

He did not see them again that day.

Turning north, he rode for hours and hours, making a wide swing to the east. As it began to get dark he was sure he was nearing Peryton.

Bob Flagg was scared to death. Lem Bowman would have killed him! With Howie at his heels, he galloped his horse across the railroad tracks and into the night.

After a mile he reined in, looking back. No one had come after them, and he took a long breath of relief. Where the hell had Bowman come from—out of the blue!

With a peculiar look on his face Howie said, "I thought you shot Matt Moody."

"I did, dammit!"

"Then why you runnin' from him—who was 'at, any-ways?"

132

"Lem Bowman. He's a killer. You seen how he shot at me—never give me a chance!"

Howie grunted. He had never really believed that story about Moody, and now he doubted it even more. Flagg would run from a vicious rabbit. But he said nothing.

Flagg gazed around them. "There ain't nothing out here but prairie dogs. But there's plenty of towns along the railroad, and we need money bad."

That was true. They were poor as country democrats. Maybe they could hold up one of the railroad workers on payday.

But Flagg thought higher than that. He said, "What we need is some rich passengers." He grinned at the other. "We could take us a sack and go through a passenger car."

"Damn dangerous—only two of us."

Flagg made a face. "One stands guard while the other grabs the wallets and jewelry. Hell, it ought to be easy."

Howie shook his head. "What if the train starts up while we's doing that?"

"Then we jump off."

"You never robbed a train, did you? We need more men for that kinda job."

"More men!" Flagg glared at him. "What for?"

"We need one'r two so they can climb up to the engine cab and make sure the train don't go nowhere till we tell it to."

Flagg growled. "That means more splits, dammit!"

"But it's safer. Besides, don't you know about the Rico Brothers?"

"What about 'em?" Flagg grinned evilly. "They got caught, as I remember."

"Yeah, maybe, but they was good train robbers before the law got 'em. We could do it like they did."

Flagg was curious. "How you mean?"

"Two got on the train, dressed like passengers. A few miles out of town—wherever they decide—they pull the cord and stop the train."

"What cord?"

"Ain't you ever been on a train? There's a cord—anyway, they pull it, and the train stops where the other two members of the gang is waiting with horses. Two of 'em keeps the train people quiet while the other two robs the passengers. Then they all gets away on the horses, slick as ice."

Flagg nodded, considering. There was a lot to know about robbing a train. And it did sound good. Robbing a passenger car full of traveling folks—who were likely to have traveling money—was a hell of a lot better than holding up some poor soul who staggers out of a saloon. And if Howie was right, the odds of getting caught were about the same.

But where were they going to find two more men willing to be train robbers?

Matt and Lem got the herd moving, but on the third day Matt knew they had gone about it in too much of a hurry. Two men were not nearly enough to do everything that needed doing. Riding, looking after the horses, cooking . . . and to begin with, neither of them had worked as cowhands for a very long time.

Matt's original plan was to hurry the beeves along, but he soon realized it would be better on him and Lem to let them graze as they went. It was slow as hell, but easier in the long run.

Night was the worst part. They took turns, one man slept as the other walked his horse around the bedded-down cows. But they both knew that if there was trouble they would likely lose the herd and the horses. Neither of them got enough sleep.

By the fourth day out they were both tired to death, nodding in the saddles. Trailing this little herd, Matt thought, was one of the worst ideas to which he had ever agreed. But they had to stick it out now.

Then a little bit of luck stumbled their way. They came to a small, round, grassy valley and circled the herd into it. They gathered wood for the fire and stayed two days, catching up on their sleep.

134

Chapter Twenty

LAREDO joined Pete on the boardwalk in front of the Wild Horse Saloon in Peryton. Seven riders had just come into town and were getting down, obviously tired; they had apparently come a long way.

A bystander asked, "You gents a posse?"

One shook his head. "We hunting a man who shot two of our friends down in Biggars."

"What's 'is name?"

"Don't know. He's kind of skinny and got a beard, and he come this way."

Another of the riders said, "We lost 'im a while back. He maybe went to ground somewheres near."

"Lots of people got beards. . . ."

The rider said, "I'll know this one, I see him again." He went into the saloon with his friends.

Laredo said softly to Pete. "A beard. I never considered that."

"T.R. with a beard?"

"It's logical." Laredo pushed through the saloon doors and sat down by one of the riders. "This man you're after—why'd he shoot your friends?"

"It was over a saloon gal. He had the money to keep her to hisself. Of course, she was the best-lookin' gal in town, and nobody liked him t'do that." The man was curious. "You think you know 'im?"

"Can't be sure, but I'll let you know what we find out."

"Thanks."

Laredo went outside again with Pete. "It sounds like T.R."

"It does, but why would he lead that bunch back here?"

Laredo grinned. "Because the money is stashed somewhere in this area."

"Dammit! We've gone over that a hundred times! If it's so, why hasn't he picked it up a month ago?"

"If I knew that answer I'd have told you long ago."

Pete rolled a cigarette and licked the flap. "Of course, we don't know that it *was* T.R. they chased. None of them knew his name."

Laredo glanced around. Near the saloon door was tacked a poster with T.R.'s picture on it. As Pete watched, puffing the cigarette, Laredo drew a mustache and beard on the photograph.

"One of those men said he'd know the face again."

"That's right. I'll get him." Pete went into the saloon and came out with several of the riders. He pointed to the poster. "Is that him?"

They stared at the photo with the penciled-in beard. One of the riders said, "Yeh! That's him! That's the sombitch!"

T.R. could see no evidence that anyone had been in or about his hideaway in the rocks. He arrived while it was yet light and curled up in his blankets for several hours.

Then he went out to walk along the barbed-wire fence, peering at the distant shack. There was a fire in front of it, and he could make out the shadowy figures of several men. Nothing appeared to be changed.

He did not see any of the prowling dogs—and thought about the strychnine he had not bought. Damn that kid, Billy! He had upset a lot of plans.

But maybe they had poison at the little settlement. He would also have to get some meat, as Brody had done, and sew the poison into it so the dogs would gulp it down.

136

He'd put it out for them as soon as he was positive he could climb onto the shack roof.

Watching the next morning, he saw only two men come from the shack. They occupied themselves with various chores, and one of them threw sticks for the dogs to chase.

T.R., tired of lying in the brush, crawled back to saddle his horse. He rode to the settlement and was disappointed. The grocer had no strychnine.

"Got no call for it, mister. Don't keep no poisons at all. Nearest place to get 'em, I 'spect, would be Peryton."

Luck was against him. He filled a sack with the supplies he needed and rode back. Did he dare go into Peryton? It had been a long time since he'd been there, since anyone in the town had seen him, and now he had grown the beard.

Besides, Matt was away with the herd. There was no way anyone could tell him that T.R. had been seen in the vicinity. He'd go in, buy the poison, and get out in a hurry.

They took a room in Peryton's only hotel, and that night at supper Laredo said, "T.R.'s come back to the Moody farm. It can't be anything else, can it?"

"Well, it doesn't have to be the farm itself. He left it in a hurry, as far as we know. Maybe he's interested in the vicinity of the farm."

"The money sack is not very big. I wonder if it could have been camouflaged?"

"You mean behind a tree?"

"Maybe."

Pete shook his head. "He had no time for that."

"He might have had more time than we think. Maybe he planned ahead."

"If he had all that time why didn't he head for New Orleans with the sack? And anyhow, what could he have made it look like that wouldn't have been investigated by now?"

Laredo sighed. "That's true. But dammit, he *is* back here, according to those men. That farm is not so small. Maybe he stumbled on a hiding place. . . ."

Pete shook his head. "He should have picked up the money a long time ago. Why didn't he?"

"What if he dropped it into a deep hole—and now he can't get it out?"

Pete smiled broadly. "That's it! That could be the answer!"

"What kind of a hole would it be?"

Pete made a face. "It's your hole. You dreamed it up. You tell me."

Laredo chuckled. "All right, let's go look for it in the morning."

But as they approached the farm next morning they came to a barbed-wire fence. In the distance they could see cattle and calves grazing. To get onto the Moody land they would have to ask permission—or cut the wire.

They rode south, paralleling the wire, and searched the route they supposed T.R. had taken to go to Loudon.

And found nothing.

Matt Moody and Lem got the herd started again. They moved out of the little valley and trailed north, the herd grazing as it went. On the second day out they saw cattle in the far distance.

Lem said, "I wonder if they's branded."

"Go take a look."

Lem rode that way and when he returned, hours later, he said, "Most unbranded critters. We could pick up a few."

"Did you see anyone?"

"No. Nobody around."

"Be too goddamn bad if they drifted over thisaway and got mixed in with ours."

They halted the herd at a wide water hole and rounded up the distant cows and yearlings, cutting out all that were branded. It took more than a day, but they increased their herd by well over a hundred head.

When they reached Sidley at last and penned the cattle and tallied them, they had nine hundred and eighty-two. A cattle

138

buyer gave them eight dollars a head, which totaled more than seven thousand dollars.

"And damn little risk," Lem said.

"But a hell of a lot of trouble," Matt said sourly. The drive over, he bought a bottle of whiskey and got good and drunk. Lem took his gun away and kept him in the hotel room, sobering him up enough two days later to get him on a horse headed back toward Peryton.

T.R. slipped into Peryton late in the afternoon, hat pulled down low. He waited patiently in the general store till several women customers cleared out, then he asked for strychnine and tobacco.

He went out to the horse and headed down a side street out of town—but one of the seven riders spotted him. He yelled, pulled a gun, and sent five shots after a racing T.R.

The chase was on again.

But by the time the riders were out of the saloon and mounted T.R. was a mile away, out of sight and galloping the horse like the wind. He was in territory he knew well, and night was coming on.

He doubled back and waited in a copse of trees, watching the group thunder past him. Then he moved west at a comfortable walk in the gathering dusk.

He never saw them again.

The seven eventually straggled back to town in the dark and held a council of war that night. They decided they could spend no more time on the chase; they all had jobs to go back to. They had given it their best and had come up empty. They went back in the morning.

T.R. knew nothing of this and stayed away for more than a week. He circled around and pointed for Hayestown, where he shaved his beard, bedded some of the painted gals, and relaxed a bit. He still had plenty of money in his saddlebags.

But Frank Griff, in Camp Hill, had repeated what Marty Nevers had told him about T.R.'s double cross, and the information found its way to Hayestown. The people in those lawless burgs were disinclined to enjoy the company of a double-crosser, for obvious reasons, and several stalked T.R.

As he came out of the Wild Boar Saloon one night, they ambushed him. T.R. probably would have been killed had it not been night, and if he had not been so agile. He jumped into the midst of tethered horses and fired back, until men came running from several saloons, and the bushwhackers disappeared.

T.R. knew they were probably men trying to score points with Matt Moody. He left town that same night and went back to his rocky hideaway near the Moody farm.

Chapter Twenty-one

Laredo and Pete had wired the United States Marshal concerning Marty Nevers, and the marshal's deputies, five in number, showed up at the farmhouse to demand his surrender.

Marty, on crutches, happened to be in the barn when the deputies shouted to him to come out. "We got the house surrounded!"

Marty threw a saddle on a roan horse, scrambled aboard, and walked the animal through the rear door of the barn and across a narrow field to the trees. He got clear away and headed for Camp Hill.

The deputies shot up the house and when they finally entered, found it vacant.

Sam was far off in the south fields digging postholes when they confronted him. He said, "Whut you all want wi' me? I ain't done nothing."

"You know where Marty Nevers is at?"

Sam shook his head. "Ain't he in the house?"

"No."

"Then I dunno any more'n you do, sah. He was there this mornin'."

"Where's he likely to go?"

Sam knew about Camp Hill and Hayestown, but he made his face blank. "Mr. Marty, he never tells me nothing."

They rounded up the two young cowhands who knew no

more than Sam. They both swore Sam had been in the field all day, and besides, Marty never talked to them. They hardly knew what he looked like.

Marty arrived in Camp Hill just before midnight, but the Lonestar Saloon was open, and fat Frank Griff was lolling in his big leather chair as usual.

Marty entered, limping badly, and fell into a chair near Griff, who was surprised to see him. "What's the matter wi' your leg? Where'd you drop from, Marty?"

"Law's after me. Thought I'd lay up here a spell."

"They foller you here?"

Marty shook his head, wincing. The damn leg hurt.

Griff frowned at the bandages. "What happened?"

"Got in the way of a bullet over in Fairview. Is there a doc in town?"

Griff nodded. "If he's sober. Are you hurtin'?"

"Yeah, a little bit."

Griff yelled at one of the bartenders and told him to go get Doc Flinders. "If he's drunk, drop 'im in a horse trough, but git him here."

The barman nodded and pulled off his apron.

Marty said, "Thanks, Frank."

Griff waved his hand. "What about T.R.? You catch 'im yet?"

"No, not yet."

Griff leaned closer. "Heard he was seen over to Hayestown not long ago."

"He was? Hayestown?"

Griff nodded. "Didn't you say he stole a pile of money from you all?"

"He sure as hell did!"

"Then what's he doing in Hayestown?"

Marty shook his head, frowning. That *was* curious as hell. Nobody went to Hayestown or Camp Hill to have a spree. They went there to hide out or make themselves scarce. Of course, there were girls and whiskey to be had, but nothing like the big towns. A man with a hundred and fifty thousand dollars in his kick would be a fool to take it to an outlaw town. He'd never get out alive with it—if anyone guessed.

Griff said, "You sure he got the money?"

"We figger he did. Nobody else coulda got it. It had to be him."

"Well, somebody took a few shots at him and run him outa town, the way I heard it. Where's Matt?"

"Him and Lem took a herd to market."

Griff chuckled. "Matt herdin' cows?"

"He gits restless. I stayed at Matt's farm till the law closed in. They surrounded the house and I was in the barn." Marty laughed. "So I slid out the back and come here. They prob'ly still sittin' there, yelling at the house."

Griff nodded. "You allus had good luck, Marty. What you going to do now?"

"Get this leg looked at, then lay up and stay outa trouble. You got a place for me?"

"Hell, yeah. We'll put you in the bridal suite." He called for a bartender to bring drinks. "Where the hell's that doc?"

Bob Flagg and Howie rode west, following the railroad tracks to Sollmon, discovering it to be a busy town, wagons and buckboards going and coming. There was a big noisy roundhouse, with a mess of sidings and a dozen boxcars waiting in the sun.

Every third building in town was a saloon, and girls yelled at them from upstairs windows as they walked the horses along the street. Flagg grinned and waved back.

"The damn place is wide open," Howie commented.

"We'll find somebody here," Flagg said, looking pleased.

It was a railroad town, and they quickly discovered it was seething. There had been a mix-up or dispute about pay, and none of the railroad employees had been paid for more than three weeks. Men were yelling and threatening in the saloons; there was talk of setting fire to the depot and the roundhouse, and calmer heads were shouted down.

It did not seem a good atmosphere to talk quietly of robbery, and Flagg was of a mind to move on.

Then Howie met Angelo.

He had a last name, he told Howie, but no one but an Italian could pronounce it. He was lean and black-haired, with a nose that obviously had been broken and casually repaired several times. He explained that he had once, when down on his luck, been a bare-knuckled saloon boxer, fighting to pass the hat—a terrible way to make a living.

"I know a better way," Howie said.

"What's that?"

"Holding up a train."

Angelo stared. "You mean robbin' the passengers—or the express car?"

"You innerested?"

The ex-boxer nodded slowly. "I got to be. I'm flat broke—or I will be if I pay my rent."

"You got a gun?"

"Yeh, but I can't hit nothing with it."

"That don't matter. If we do it right we won't have to shoot nobody."

"You ain't thinking of holding up a train—just the two of us?"

Howie shook his head. "I got a partner. Let's go talk to him."

When Matt Moody and Lem returned to the farmhouse they found it shot to pieces. There were hundreds of bullet holes in the sides of the house. All the windows were shot out, and it was a miracle the lamps had not set the place afire.

No one was inside, but Sam came running from the barn when he heard them talking. Matt growled. "What the hell happened here?"

"The law come lookin' for you, Mr. Matt."

"Where's Marty?"

"He must of seen 'em or something. He got out. Took the roan horse. I dunno where he went."

Sam had cleaned up some of the mess inside, sopped up the spilled coal oil, and swept up the shattered window glass.

144

The house was liveable. It might take a month to patch up all the bullet holes, but it was summertime, and that chore could wait.

Sam had talked to the men who had surrounded the house; they had found him in the fields and had asked him questions.

"They was five of 'em, Mr. Matt. Wearin' badges."

"Not from Peryton?"

"No sah. I never seed any of 'em before."

"Maybe the county sheriff," Lem said.

"Maybe." Matt brooded about it. "The law never come here before. You figger that sombitch T.R. put 'em up to it?"

"He prob'ly did."

Matt pulled his mustache. "It bothers the hell outa me that he went to Hayestown. If he had the money why'd he do that? We figgered he'd be in one o' them eastern cities by now."

"Well, he sure'n hell got the money. We seen where he dug it up."

Matt sighed deeply. "That's right." He poured a drink and swished the whiskey around in the glass. "You spose you coulda got held up and lost it all?"

Lem grunted. "I kinda hope he did."

"That would account for him not spendin' it." Matt gulped the liquor and made a face. "Griff said they chased him outa town. I wonder where he went. . . ."

Spud Suggins went to talk to Frank Griff. He was a skinny little bird who looked like somebody who had been eating out of trash cans most of his life. He dressed in somewhat the same fashion, and he smelled bad.

But he had something to say. He had happened to be in the right place at the right time, he told Griff.

"Where was that?"

"In Sollmon. That's a railroad town. One of the telegraphers let me sleep in a corner of the office under some old blankets. I was there when his relief come on, and he didn't notice me." He paused.

145

"Yeah," Griff said. "Go on."

"You a fair man, Frank. Ever'body says so."

"What?" Griff frowned.

Spud cowered at his look. "I—I ain't expectin' much, Frank. . . ."

"Oh—money. You want money, is that it?"

Spud nodded. "I got somethin' to sell, ain't I?"

"I dunno what it is yet. I'm listenin'."

Spud fingered his torn shoes, head down.

Griff said, "All right, Spud. You give me something I c'n use, and you get money. I'm a fair man."

Spud brightened. "Well, they was a message come over the wire. Them railroad people ain't been paid for a long time. The message said the money was comin' on the next train."

"When's that?"

"About six days."

"Six days from when?"

"Yesterday."

"Did they say how much money?"

"There was something about a hunnerd thousand. They sendin' it in a special express car from Kansas City. Nobody's sposed to know."

"Is that all of it?"

"All I know, Frank."

Griff reached in a pocket and drew out a roll of greenbacks. He peeled off five and handed them over. "Thanks, Spud."

When the little man had gone, he sent for Marty Nevers.

Marty limped in half an hour later, and they sat with their heads together as Griff outlined what Spud had told him. Griff also had a map of the railroad system and spread it out on his ample knees.

He tapped the paper. "You get on the train at Quigley, right here. It's a water stop. The money will be in the express car."

"How many guards?"

"Spud didn't know. I'd guess three, maybe four, but nobody's supposed to know about the shipment, so maybe only two."

Marty frowned over the map.

Griff said, "You uncouple the express car and send the rest of the train on. Then you can take your time about it."

"Them guards going to barricade themselves in the car."

"Sure. But you build a fire under it, and they'll come out."

"We don't want to burn up the money."

Griff shrugged. "It'll be in a strongbox. Soon's the guards come out, you put out the fire. You got a tank of water right handy." He called a bartender for paper and a pencil.

Marty said, "We gotta get somebody to open the strongbox. How we going to do that?"

"There'll be a express man in the car with the guards. There's horses and mules at Quigley. You ride back here, and we'll split."

"What's your cut?"

"Fifteen percent." Griff accepted the paper and pencil and wrote a note and sealed it up. He gave it back to the bartender with orders to have someone hustle to the Moody farm with it. "Matt and Lem will meet you at Quigley." Griff looked at Marty's leg. "You think you ought to be ridin' around with that? Maybe we should send Luke Potter instead."

"I'll get Doc Flinders to look at it."

Griff nodded.

But when Flinders examined the leg, he shook his head. "You aren't going nowhere, friend. You want to lose that leg? If gangrene sets in, it's gone."

Quigley, named for the man in charge of the station, was a water tower, two shacky houses, and a pole corral. Alongside the tracks were heavy wooden bins containing tools and materials for road gangs. The entire layout was a blot on the prairie.

Quigley lived in one of the houses, and the other was a

147

bunkhouse for the maintenance crews that showed up now and then to break the monotony.

Luke Potter met Matt and Lem at Quigley the night before the train was due. They quickly disarmed Quigley, a skinny, raw-boned gent who was astonished to see them, recognizing Matt Moody from his wanted posters. He agreed to stay in his house, happy not to be shot.

Luke explained Griff's plan: Uncouple the express car and get rid of the engine and passenger cars, then take their time about getting the men out of the express car.

Matt agreed it was a good plan. He especially liked the part about setting the car afire.

Chapter Twenty-two

Laredo said, "T.R. came back here for a reason. He came back for the money."

"You said he dropped it into a deep hole."

"And it might be there. He could be busy digging it out, right this minute."

Pete looked beyond the barbed-wire fence. "The Moody land is pretty flat. Good for grazing or even farming, but anyone digging there would be seen very soon."

"So the money's not on the farm, but somewhere nearby."

Pete nodded. "I think so—I mean I *guess* so. But there must be some reason why he hasn't dug it up a long time ago—if he's still in one piece." He looked at Laredo. "A broken arm would be a good reason."

"Ummm. But nobody's said anything about seeing him with a broken arm."

Pete was silent a moment. "You don't suppose he *forgot* where he stashed it?"

Laredo laughed. "Forget a hundred and fifty thousand dollars! Is that possible?"

"Well, he was in a hurry. . . ."

Laredo pulled at his chin. "Ummm, yes. It could be, I suppose. But surely by now he's retraced his steps a hundred times, looking for it."

"Let's us do some more looking." Pete sighed. "Maybe we'll get lucky and stumble over it."

* * *

Howie stole a grain sack from the local livery and rolled it up under his arm as they walked to the depot.

On the platform Flagg said, "We don't have any money for tickets."

Howie and Angelo stared at him in surprise. "Jesus! We're gonna hold up the damn train! Why do we need tickets?"

Flagg sighed and grunted at them.

They paced nervously, staying away from other people, but the train was nearly on time. It clamored into the station, hissing steam as bells tolled: an engine with a tall spark stack, a wood car, three passenger cars, an express car, and caboose.

Howie said, "Let's get on the last car."

He led the way up the steps onto the open platform with its light iron railing and looked at the express car.

The car had a stout, metal-sheathed door that appeared to be locked on the inside.

Angelo said, "They prob'ly got a secret knock—or they don't open it to nobody."

Flagg frowned at him. "You done this before?"

"No, but that's the way I'd do it."

Howie opened the passenger car door, and they entered and sat in the last seats. The car was only half-full.

Flagg said, "All right, we hold them up as soon's the train gets started. They put their goods in the grain sack, and we all get off at Quigley."

"That's right," Angelo nodded. "Howie takes the sack, and me and you hold our guns on 'em."

"We go through all three cars," Flagg said.

"Why don't we get what's in the express car instead?" Howie asked.

"We dint plan it that way," Flagg growled.

"But there's likely more in the express car and without all that trouble."

The conductor appeared at the other end of the car, and the train jerked, moved, and jerked again, and then the station started to slide by. The conductor, a slim man with a

150

white mustache, stood talking with several passengers. Then he came down the aisle toward them.

Flagg pulled his Colt and held it under his coat, glancing at the others. When the conductor asked for tickets they would rise and confront him.

But he went past them without a look, opened the rear door, and stepped onto the open platform. Howie jumped up at once and peered through the grimy glass of the door.

Then he turned and whispered to them, "He knocked like this." He motioned with his closed fist. "And they opened the door."

Angelo hissed, "Let's do the same thing!"

Howie's eyes were shining. "The express car's better'n robbing the passengers."

Flagg gave in. He crowded onto the tiny open platform with them. Howie glanced back, grinning, then he rapped hard on the door.

It opened immediately, and a face glared at them. Howie pushed his pistol at the man—and the express guard fired through the open door.

Howie slumped to the platform, and Angelo fired as fast as he could thumb the hammer, pushing into the car. Someone inside fired shots at the door, splintering it and smashing into the ceiling. The car filled with smoke. Angelo and Flagg were lying atop Howie's body, firing into the car—and then suddenly it was still.

Angelo crawled into the car. "They dead, three of 'em."

The conductor and two others were shot. Howie was dead, also. Flagg lifted the body and shoved it off the platform. Too bad about Howie . . .

Behind him Angelo said, "There's a strongbox here. Might be something important in it."

Flagg closed the door. In a moment someone hammered on it from the other side. He said, "They heard the shootin'."

Angelo opened the big side door and peered out. "Let's dump out the strongbox and jump. There's nothin' else in here."

"Yeah." Flagg looked at the ceiling. They'll climb up

151

there in a minute or two, he thought. He helped Angelo push the strongbox out and watched it thump and tumble down the slight slope. Angelo stood in the doorway, then hesitated. The train rattled over a trestle, and he looked down fifty feet to a creek bed.

Flagg swore, looking back to where the safe had tumbled down. The track curved as the train left the trestle, and below them was a rocky cut.

"We can't jump into that," Angelo said, growling.

"But the strongbox is a mile back already!"

"Then you jump."

Flagg leaned out. Looking ahead he could see that the land was leveling out again. The rails were above the prairie; it was a grassy slope. Angelo said, "Now!"

He jumped out, and Flagg followed. When he hit, it knocked the breath out of him. He bumped and rolled to the bottom of the slope and lay, gasping and hurting. He felt bruised all over—but nothing was broken. He stared at the sky, then sat up wearily to see the train disappearing, black smoke from the engine stack staining the sky.

Angelo said, "You all right?"

"I think so." Flagg managed to get to his feet, groaning. He brushed dirt from his clothes and took a few halting steps.

Angelo said, "That strongbox must be back there five miles or more."

Flagg looked at him. "When we find it, can we open it?"

Angelo sighed. "Jeez, I never thought of that."

The train came along the tracks slowly and halted at the Quigley water tower. Matt held out his arm; something was wrong. "Wait a minute. . . ."

The side door of the express car was wide open, and several trainmen were moving about inside. A crowd of passengers got off the train, talking excitedly in groups. Matt and the others listened. There had been a holdup and a lot of shooting. The conductor and two others were dead. The strongbox was missing.

Matt said softly, "Somebody got to it before us."

"Some secret," Lem said sourly.

Luke said, "Let's ride back along the tracks."

"We won't find nothing." Lem shook his head. "This here was planned good. They'll be forty miles away by the time we find out where they stole the strongbox—if we find it."

"Let's give it a try, anyways," Matt said. He mounted and turned toward the tracks. The others followed.

It took the rest of the day for Flagg and Angelo to walk back to where they thought they'd dumped out the strongbox. It looked different than it had from the train. It was in a dense, brushy area, and they pushed through the brush till darkness overtook them.

Angelo said in a tired voice, "Maybe there's nothing inside it, anyways."

"They always carry money and treasure in the safe. That's why they had guards."

"But if we can't open it, what good is it?"

"Wait'll we find it."

"But we can't carry it nowhere neither. We got no horses. We're afoot, dammit, Flagg!"

It had all gone sour, Flagg thought disgustedly. Who's idea was it anyway, robbing a train? They should have stuck to the first plan, robbing passengers and getting away at Quigley where there were horses. It had been Howie who pushed at them to go into the express car. That damn fool, Howie! And now he was dead. It damn well served him right!

They had nothing to eat or drink and no blankets. They made themselves as comfortable as possible in the brush and spent a miserable night.

In the early morning Angelo said, "Them train people is going to send others out to look for the strongbox. We better find it first."

"They won't know where to look."

"No, but they could send out a dozen men or more."

That was true, Flagg reflected. The railroad had lots of

153

men. It wouldn't take them long to search every foot of the tracks.

But they found where the heavy strongbox had furrowed the earth, and Angelo gave a shout. The strongbox was in a clump of brush, upside down. They levered it out, and Flagg grabbed the handle. It was locked.

"We'd need dynamite to open that damn thing!"

Angelo kicked it. "We got to take it to a locksmith."

"How? We got no wagon."

"We'll hide it and come back for it with a wagon."

"Yeah, good idea." Flagg looked around. "Where we going to hide it?"

"Let's see if we can lift it first."

They got their hands under it, grunted, and were able to lift it waist-high. Angelo motioned with his head. "Over there. Get it away from the tracks as far's we can."

They walked toward a section of ground that was humped and furrowed, and beyond it was an arroyo. Grunting and straining, they staggered into the shallow arroyo and dropped the heavy box.

Flagg sat on it. "Now what? We can't hide this thing very easy. It's too big."

The arroyo curved away from the tracks, and Angelo started along it. "Let's look for a place."

They walked half a mile and found a niche that looked as if it would do. They went back for the strongbox and managed to get it to the niche by resting and staggering and resting again.

With knives they pulled dirt over it, then scattered leaves and branches over the place till they were satisfied it might pass a casual inspection.

Angelo climbed out of the arroyo and studied the lay of the land. "We got to be sure we can find this place again."

There were no natural landmarks. Flagg said, "It ain't far from that trestle."

"That's right—a mile or two east of it. It'll have to do."

They were tired and hungry. Flagg said, "Now what? We follow the tracks?"

154

"The nearest town's prob'ly along the railroad. We passed a couple of whistle-stops if I remember."

Flagg sighed. "All right, let's go."

Chapter Twenty-three

THEY did not stumble over the money sack, but they flushed out a rider in a rocky section of brush and scrub pine south of the barbed-wire fence of the Moody farm. He came galloping through a stand of willows and headed south through a cover of trees.

Pete yelled, "It's T.R.!" He spurred after the other.

Laredo had had only a glimpse of the fugitive's face. If it was T.R., he had shaved off the beard. He followed Pete.

They managed to keep the distant rider in view for several hours, but lost him when darkness fell. They reined in and got down to make camp.

Laredo said, "We must have come close to his hideout. He didn't wait for us to knock on his door."

"That proves he doesn't have the money."

"But he probably knows where it is."

Pete sighed. "Down that hole you invented a little while ago?"

"It's possible."

In the morning T.R.'s tracks were distinct on the ground, leading across a long, sweeping meadow up to a straggle of jack pines on the crest. From there they could see the tiny settlement, obscured by the haze.

They lost the tracks in a marshy stretch before they reached the houses, but when Laredo showed T.R.'s photograph to the general store owner the other nodded his head.

"He been in here half a dozen times."

"When was the last?"

The man scratched his head. "A week or two maybe—he wanted some strychnine."

Laredo looked at Pete. "Poison?"

Pete asked, "What did he want strychnine for?"

"He didn't say. I told him he could maybe get it over to Peryton."

They thanked the man and went out to the horses. "Poison?" Laredo said again.

Pete grinned. "Maybe to poison Matt Moody and the others."

"You can't poison people with strychnine, can you? It's so bitter no one would eat it."

Pete said innocently, "Depends on how hungry you are."

"Of course. I should have thought of that."

Evidently T.R. had not come into the little settlement but had gone around. They picked up his trail beyond, and it led them over the desert flats and down into a dusty valley and the town of Biggars.

He had been riding a bay horse, and it seemed, as they rode down the main street, that every third or fourth horse was a bay.

Laredo said, "Did he stop here or go on?"

"He stopped," Pete said definitely. "He didn't have time to put together any supplies. He'll try to get them here."

They wired John Fleming first thing, bringing him up to date. They were tracking T.R., whom they suspected of knowing where the reservation money was hidden. Fleming had no news or information for them. His instruction was simple: "Take him alive."

They then showed the photograph to three store owners, and all shook their heads; they had not seen him. Two livery stable owners said the same thing: "Ain't seen him."

Two hotel clerks also turned down the corners of their mouths. He had not taken a room in either hotel. There were several dozen boardinghouses in town, and it might take a week to look into each one. They decided to visit the saloons first.

Three bartenders looked at the photograph and said "No, I ain't seen him." But the fourth studied the photo carefully then nodded. "Yeh, he been in here."

"Recently?" Laredo asked.

"Yesterday," the barman said.

Matt Moody, Lem, and Luke Potter rode east from Quigley along the steel rails, looking for any indication that a heavy metal strongbox had been pushed off the train. They were looking for a fresh gash in the earth, Matt said, and maybe a plain trail where the heavy safe had smashed its way through the brush.

Privately, Luke thought it was a fool's errand, though he dared not use that particular term to Matt. He said, "Whoever broke into the express car had a wagon waiting, sure'n hell. It don't make no sense otherwise."

Lem was inclined to agree. Maybe the robbers had forced the expressman to open the strongbox before shooting him.

Matt said it didn't look that way to him. A wagon would have left tracks.

It was slow going, looking at every inch of ground on both sides of the tracks. The second day out, they came to a high trestle bridge over a dry wash. The sides were steep shelf rock, and it took an hour to find a way down, then more trouble getting up the other side.

When they finally reached the tracks again, Luke had had enough. "I goin' back to Camp Hill. You all can have my share."

Matt only shrugged and made no objection.

A strong wind came up that day, and they rode into it, heads down. They did not find any gash in the earth, or wagon tracks, and rode all the way to the next town, Fillmore. It was a tired-looking, dusty burg, a whistle-stop with a tent saloon.

Over a beer Matt said, "We been playin' in hard luck ever since T.R. took off with that money. I figger it jinxed us."

"It sure ain't done us any good."

"We got to get back to banks. Quit foolin' around with that damn railroad."

Lem nodded. "Mebbe so."

"Marty oughta be able to ride pretty soon."

"Yeh, he ought to."

"Then we c'n git back into business." Matt sipped the beer. "When we get back to the farm I'm goin' to sell the rest of them cows. Maybe even sell the farm."

"You don't need it."

"That's right, not no more." He sighed and finished the beer. "Let's git outa here."

The railroad sent out a squad of detectives armed with descriptions of the three men who had sat in the back of the passenger car nearest the express car. Those three, according to other passengers, had held up the express car and killed the conductor and others.

They quickly discovered the body of Howie in the brush and tracked down Bob Flagg and Angelo, taking them into the Fillmore jail where they were questioned separately.

Angelo admitted nothing. When he was hustled to the undertaker's rooms to view the body, he stated he did not know Howie: "He's a stranger to me."

Others swore they had seen him with Howie on the train. Angelo said he had not held up the express car and did not know where the strongbox was. He admitted knowing Flagg but said they had just met. He knew nothing about Flagg. He said it all very convincingly.

McNab, the railroad detective in charge, did not believe a word of it.

When he questioned Flagg he first said, "You're going to spend the next twenty years behind bars in the territorial prison—and I assure you it ain't a nice place to live. That is, if the judge don't give you the rope."

Flagg almost cried. "But I didn't do nothing!"

"The hell you didn't. You shot them people on the train and stole the strongbox."

159

"No, no, no."

"Tell us where the money is, and it'll go easier on you."

Flagg looked hopeful. "It will? How much easier?"

McNab frowned at him. "It might save you from the rope. You'll still go to jail."

Flagg felt his neck.

"Your friend, Angelo, has already told us all about it, you know."

Flagg stared at the big detective. Angelo had turned against him?

McNab said, "He says you were the leader of the gang."

"I was not! He was the leader!"

"No, I think he's tellin' the truth. You were the leader."

"He's a liar!" Flagg was red in the face. "It was his idea to hold up the express car. His and Howie's. I just went along because I was broke."

"I see. And where is the money?"

Flagg became suspicious. "I thought you said Angelo already told you."

McNab smiled. "We like to hear all sides. He may not be telling the truth about it. Where's the strongbox, Flagg?"

Flagg pressed his lips together, scowling.

McNab stared at him a moment then went to the cell door and yelled to a jailer: "Come in here, Willie, and bring that rubber hose."

Flagg gulped. "Wait a minute. . . ."

"You change your mind?"

"If I t-tell you where the money is—will that c-count in my favor?"

"Oh yes, it certainly will."

Flagg sighed deeply. "All right. It's in an arroyo, covered over with dirt and leaves, about one or two miles east of the trestle."

McNab smiled and went out.

T.R. had been surprised by the sudden appearance of the two mounted men near his hideout. They seemed to be coming directly toward his position. He must have been dozing in the sun. He caught a glimpse of them as he slid away toward the rope corral where his bay horse waited. It was the big blond man and the Mexican. Were they the law?

He bridled the bay, grabbed up a blanket, then swung the saddle onto the horse's back. He had no time to pack a food sack. If he was lucky he could get out by a back way before they saw him. He stepped up and dug in the spurs. They would chase him, of course, but he knew every inch of the country, and probably they did not.

But he was unable to lose them. They stuck like glue across the plains and into the far hills that were stippled with dark shadows. He bypassed the little settlement and headed for Biggars where he could get food.

Biggars was an old town with wind-scarred adobes and a hundred sun-bleached shacks, many of them occupied. T.R. moved into an empty one, horse and all.

He was able to watch his two pursuers approach the town. They were probably deputies or Pinkertons. How had they known where to look for him? Could they be employed by Matt Moody? No, not very likely.

He stayed hidden, except in the late evening when he slipped out afoot and bought food at a general store far from the center of town, just before it closed for the night. He sat in the hut and ate ravenously.

He ought to return to the farm as soon as possible. He had the strychnine now, in his saddlebags; he was ready to make his move for the money sack. He had waited long enough. Anyone who stood in his way now—too bad. Maybe he would leave here tomorrow night. Give the bay a good rest.

He finished a can of cold beans and ate half a loaf of bread, wishing for hot coffee. Damn! He was putting up with a lot! When he had the money, things were going to change!

He leaned against the wall of the old shack and dreamed again about the money. He'd never have to work again. He wouldn't throw it around carelessly; he'd put it in an eastern bank and live like a gentleman. He'd read about gentlemen, seen pictures of them. They wore fine clothes and drank the best wines—he didn't care much for wine, though. Most of

161

what he'd had had been bitter. He preferred beer. But a gentleman could drink beer—hell, if he had the money, who was there to tell him what he could drink?

He thought about beer. He could slip into a saloon tonight, a small one—there must be twenty saloons in town—and have a beer. It had been a while. . . .

And it was easy. He had two beers and went back to the hut.

He slept late the next morning. The bay had a small saddle sore, and he decided to wait one more day before going back.

That night he studied the sky, dark with no moon. Perfect. He'd go to the saloon and have one more beer, then he'd go.

He walked toward the main street.

Chapter Twenty-four

THE saloon had a badly lettered sign out front that read: HALLEY'S PLACE. The bat-wing doors squeaked as they entered. It was a deadfall with a puncheon floor, a few card tables, and a long, well-used, battered bar that had no rail but a wooden step. The room was low-ceilinged, with half a dozen heavy black lanterns hanging from hooks. There was a wide mirror over the back bar, with glasses stacked in front of it. Near the top of the mirror was a .45-caliber hole with dozens of line cracks extending from it in every direction.

Laredo and Pete sat at one of the tables at the side of the room with beer mugs before them. Pete fished out the makin's and rolled a cigarette expertly. If T.R. had showed up here yesterday, he might come again.

It was late in the evening, and there were fifteen or twenty men scattered about the room, drinking and gabbing, some playing cards. There were no women, and no one was at the piano.

Pete said, "You don't suppose we're wasting our time here? He might go back to the farm."

Laredo nodded. "I was wondering the same thing."

"The money's hidden in that hole in the ground."

"You might be right." Laredo pushed back his hat. "He led us here hoping we'd go on south."

"While he circled back."

Laredo sipped the beer and looked at it critically. "It must be a damn deep hole. Maybe an old mine shaft."

Pete nodded. "That's why he hasn't been able to reach it in all this time."

"It could be."

Pete lit the cigarette and puffed.

And then T.R. walked in the door.

He came in slowly, looking around as if he expected to find snakes on the floor. He stood where the lantern light did not reach him, and Pete nudged Laredo.

"It's him."

Casually, Laredo pulled his hat brim down. T.R. was examining every person in the room, and when his gaze came to the two of them, Laredo thought he stiffened.

Then he turned and went out to the street.

"He saw us," Laredo said, getting up. He hurried to the door with Pete at his heels. A shot smashed the wood beside the door as they slid out into the dark. T.R. was running down the street.

Laredo drew his pistol and fired a shot over the running man's head. He had no desire to kill T.R.—but how to stop him? He saw the other look back, his face a pale blur in the night, then T.R. slid to a halt and fired four times.

Pete and Laredo hit the dirt, and T.R. ran to the right as Pete fired, his bullet raising dust under T.R.'s legs.

They got up and ran after him. T.R. had crossed a vacant, weedy lot to an alley. Laredo motioned, and they separated. When they started across the lot T.R. fired at them again, his bullets rapping into the building over Laredo's head.

Pete aimed below the muzzle flashes and fired again, but when they reached the alley T.R. was far down it. He turned and fired once more, and the bullet smashed a fence post at Laredo's elbow.

They jogged along the alley, but T.R. had disappeared. He had gone between two of the houses or shacks. It was dark and shadowy, and they moved cautiously, stopping to listen. They were on the edge of town. He couldn't have gone far.

"He's in one of these shacks," Pete said softly.

Laredo nodded. Probably.

Then, a dozen yards to their left, a wide door was flung open, and a horse and rider exploded from the building. T.R. was hunched over the mount's back. He saw them at once and began firing.

Laredo dropped to the ground and fired back . . . and saw the rider violently thrown out of the saddle. T.R. slammed into the ground, and the horse ran off, waggling its head.

When they reached him, T.R. was dead.

Matt Moody and Lem went back to the farm near Peryton. The house was empty. Where was Marty?

Matt said, "He could be in Camp Hill. Maybe he got tired o' waitin' for us."

"Could be. Reckon I ought to go git him? You'll be selling them cows."

"Yeh. Good idea." Matt went out to the porch. "I'll go into Peryton in the mornin'. Ought to arrange a sale pretty easy." He stepped to the ground and looked at the house. "Needs a coat of paint."

"Whitewash it."

"Naw, paint's better." Matt shaded his eyes and looked south. "Ought to pull down that old shack, too. Goddamn eyesore. I'll have Sam burn the sombitch. Make the place look better."

Lem grunted. Land was cheap as hell. Matt wasn't going to get much for it. Maybe he wanted to sell it because it reminded him of his mother—or did Matt have such feelings?

He got together some food in a grain sack. In the morning he'd saddle up and ride to Camp Hill.

The town marshal and the undertaker arrived at nearly the same moment. The marshal, a stout man with a matchstick in the corner of his mouth, looked at the body, listened to what they had to say, and examined their credentials. Then he nodded to the black-clad undertaker who, with his assistant, put the body into a buckboard and drove away.

In the morning they went to the undertaking parlor with the marshal. T.R.'s identity was quickly established. The marshal had brought along several Wanted dodgers and compared them with the body laid out on the metal table.

"That's Toby Rogers, all right. Guess you git the reward, gents."

There was more than fifty dollars in T.R.'s jeans; plenty to pay for the burial and a painted coffin. It was doubtless stolen money, but so long as the county did not have to pay for the funeral, no one mentioned it.

"He had a horse, too," Laredo said, and the marshal nodded and promised he would have some men look for it.

They went to the telegraph office and were told the line was down, not an unusual occurrence. They rode back to Peryton to send a wire to John Fleming. Another of the Moody gang was dead. They hadn't wanted to kill him, but he had made it very difficult for himself to stay alive. Fleming was unhappy about it, too, worrying that the last chance at the reservation money had gone glimmering.

But T.R. had been an outlaw and a killer, and no one would miss him—unless it was a saloon girl somewhere who might shed a single tear.

They rode to the place where they had flushed T.R. out and quickly found his hideaway. It was a comfortable camping spot in the rocks, with a stout lean-to and plenty of airtights. They made a fire and spent the night.

But in the morning they discovered no hole in the ground, no mine shaft, or any other hiding place.

Pete growled. "He didn't have the money."

"He must have stayed here for a reason."

"You still think he knew where the money was and couldn't get at it?"

Laredo shrugged. "Don't you?"

"Yes, but it's impossible."

They wired Fleming again that the money was probably lost forever. All knowledge of it had probably died with T.R. They had found his hideaway, but no clues to the money.

Fleming wired back that the United States Marshal and an

army of deputies had raided Camp Hill and rounded up a hundred Wanted people, including Marty Nevers and Lem Bowman. They would be questioned and maybe knew something about the money. And they would stand trial for their crimes.

Then Fleming asked: "Where is Matt Moody?"

They rode back to the farm and found him on the front porch, sitting in a chair with a bottle of whiskey on the porch rail in front of him.

As they turned in from the road, Moody fumbled out his pistol and yelled at them, "What you want?"

They separated as he fired at them, getting clumsily to his feet.

Pete shouted, "He's drunk."

Moody emptied the pistol, mostly into the sky, then fell over the chair as he attempted to run into the house. Laredo took the gun away, and they tied his hands behind his back. He was bleary-eyed drunk. They hauled him inside and tossed him onto the bed, then tied his feet as he swore at them.

"The hired man ought to be around somewhere," Laredo said. "Let's put Moody in the buckboard and take him into town."

Sam was not in the barn. They climbed onto the horses and rode across the fields and found him at the old shack. Sam was using a mule to pull down the shack and was piling the wood to be burned.

He looked around as they approached. "Mr. Matt wants this here shack down. He sold all the cows, and he goin' to sell the property."

Laredo leaned on the saddle horn. "Mr. Matt is going to federal prison. I'm afraid you're out of a job, Sam."

Sam stared at them. "You lawmen, huh?"

"That's right."

Sam put his hat on and sighed deeply. He had a rope from the mule's collar to the corner of the shack. He slapped the mule's butt, and as the animal strained forward, part of the roof came crashing down. Sam went back to untie the rope.

Pete said, *"Dios Mio!"* He pointed.

Laredo looked and got down. A stained, brown canvas bag was poking up in the middle of the crumpled black tar paper. He pulled the sack out. Across it in black letters were the words: PROPERTY OF THE U.S. GOVERNMENT.

"It's been there on the roof all this time," Pete said, letting his breath out. "There's your mine shaft."

About the Author

Arthur Moore is the author of sixteen Westerns, including five previous titles in the Bluestar Western series, published by Fawcett Books. He lives in Westlake Village, California.